LOVE IT WHEN YOU COME,
HATE IT WHEN YOU GO

LOVE IT WHEN YOU COME, HATE IT WHEN YOU GO

STORIES

SHARON LEACH

PEEPAL TREE

First published in Great Britain in 2014
Peepal Tree Press Ltd
17 King's Avenue
Leeds LS6 1QS
England

ISBN13: 9781845232368

Supported using public funding by
ARTS COUNCIL
ENGLAND

CONTENTS

For Mummy

We walk through ourselves, meeting robbers, ghosts, giants, old men, young men, wives, widows, brothers-in-love, but always meeting ourselves.

— James Joyce, *Ulysses*

FIFTEEN MINUTES

An agent was the only way to go, for bookings and everything else. All the big stars had agents. Even the no-name ones. She would become a big-time Hollywood star; she'd always dreamed that. Right now, talk shows were interested. That was fine. But that was just the tip of the iceberg; she craved more – celebrity product endorsements – hell, maybe even national ad campaigns for make-up, perfume, lingerie. Fast food, well, that was iffy – depended on what kind – nothing greasy and disgusting – her skin, even at her age, was prone to acne breakouts. No biggie. She was up for anything. How did that saying go? The world was her oyster and this was the land of opportunities. For now, she would work with TV – until she could reposition herself for the big screen. All she needed was a foot in the door. In the meantime, TV. She'd worked hard with a trainer to manage her weight so that she wouldn't appear bloated – everybody knew TV added ten pounds. Right now, she needed a guest-starring role on a primetime show. Comedy or drama, she wasn't fussy. Or, better still, a reality show. She wasn't a fan but there was no denying those shows could lead to more, maybe to her own talk show. She was famous now. Well, almost. Almost famous. Ha ha. Like the movie. But look how far she'd come, from that shithole in Kingston. She had her daddy to thank for that. Thank God for DNA tests. Turned out that the man her mother had whored around with had, for whatever reason, filed for her and sent her to college. So far, she'd not managed to get out of that godforsaken North Carolina backwater, but one day everybody in Jamaica would know her name. Sheer luck had brought her to this point and she'd be an idiot not to capitalise on it. She would become a fucking celebrity. Another Kardashian.

She'd been invited to a few red carpet premieres. She'd begun to be recognised when she went out. Naturally, men had started coming on to her. She'd given head to more men in the last few months than at any other time in her life. Which said a lot since, unlike most of her girlfriends, she'd always liked giving blowjobs – most women were squeamish or they griped about jaw cramps. There'd been celebrities, too – a rapper (hitless since the 90s) who delighted in debasing her in countless ways; a famous television anchorman with a secret drug problem; a basketball star with the Knicks who was incapable of screwing her unless she dressed and spoke like a five-year-old; and a faded androgynous, middle-aged blonde R&B singer from the eighties intent on making a comeback.

But calls for bookings were slowing. She'd shelled out good money to hire an acting coach but where were the jobs? "Find me work!" she snapped at the agent, a nervous woman with big, stiff-sprayed hair. "Ah dat mi a pay you fo'". Then, into the mist of incomprehension that hovered like a mushroom cloud, she clarified, "That's what I'm paying you for. Isn't it?"

"So… I can't believe I'm here with you. You're the It-Girl, y'know? Like Paris. Lohan…"

He was beautiful and slight – nobody, really. His name wasn't a household one. But he was a model, and so he was loaded, at least on his way to becoming so.

"Yeah, well." She sipped from an oversize glass of wine, and affected a bored posture.

"I'm serious. What you did was the coolest thing, ever! Saving that kid. And with you afraid of water. Diving in – that's just awesome."

She was touched by how sincere he was, and had to fight the urge to confess that rescuing the kid, Toby, who had dived, not fallen, into the pool, had been a buck-up. That he was really an eleven-year-old on his way to a serious drug problem, who had in fact been fleeing the dealer, who operated from the back of the Y, where she'd gone to buy a dime bag of weed. That, yes, she swam like a fish, and she'd never been afraid of water. That she and Toby had promised keep each other's secret. But she bit her lip instead and continued to look bored.

She'd met the model the weekend before, at a party in New York. The week after she was on the west coast, visiting him. From where they sat in his darkened living room, the view was of mountains and sea. Behind them music quietly spilled out from his elaborate entertainment system, filling the room like a mist. They could see one of LA's most intriguing sights: a Pacific sunset merging with the blanket spread of lights that flowed from the front steps right out to the sea.

"Where have you got to, *leibling*?" the model, a blue-eyed boy with bee-stung lips, originally from Frankfurt, asked, a frown in his voice. Then stretching, so that his incredible six-pack showed beneath his shirt, he reached over, took the wine glass from her, and set it down on the glass coffee table in front of them.

She smiled, lightly flicked his muscular arm. She could scarcely believe that she was sitting here in a living room almost overlooking Beverly Boulevard. Not bad, considering she'd met him only after being rejected by a man she'd been trying to snare at that party, an important East Coast man with connections to powerful movie directors. But this would do. She smiled at him again. Maybe it was even better.

Her agent said the phones had stopped ringing for her. "We knew it wouldn't last forever, hon," she said, patting her hand across the table. "This happens all the time. They give you your fifteen minutes, then they move on. They have incredibly short memories in Hollywood."

They were at lunch at Second Ave Deli, a haunt of East Coast celebrities – bonafides and up-and-comers. Here, starlets brushed shoulders with A-listers, the beautiful anorexic set contemplated their plates of garnished celery sticks, and celebrities famous for being famous answered chirping cellphones and BlackBerrys.

She tapped her finger against her front teeth, distracted. Her agent wasn't being truthful. She'd seen ordinary people turn their fifteen minutes of fame into a Hollywood career. That girl from *Survivor*, as a for instance, had got a gig hosting on *The View* with Barbara Walters. And why hadn't she moved on that screenplay that guy had volunteered to write? Anybody could become a star. This was fucking America, wasn't it?

Around them flatware clinked. They'd been there already almost forty minutes and still nobody had recognised her. Hoisting up her sunglasses onto her head, she looked around expectantly. Still nobody ventured over for an autograph, or to snatch a bit of food off her plate to sell on eBay.

"So, how's model boy?"

"OK," she said, staring out the window. The truth was model boy had dropped her shortly after they'd gone to a party in Beverly Hills and her name hadn't shown up on the list.

"I need work." She stared despondently into her matzoh ball soup. "I'd take a non-speaking role," she said listlessly, turning to look at a man who sat scratching his nose and staring at her from a table across the room.

"Sweetie." The agent spoke soothingly, looking up from her chicken salad. She had a face that seemed composed totally of contours and planes. Her lipstick had faded, leaving the faintest trace of lip-liner. "There's nothing."

"Kim Kardashian gets paid by the hottest club owners just to show up at their clubs. Lindsay Lohan –"

"Due respect, that's Kim K and Lindsay L. A party girl and a Hollywood star. And let me tell you this. Their bubble will burst soon. Nobody's hot forever."

Why was the agent fighting her like this? William Hung was still milking his wretched Ricky Martin impression, still turning up on goddamned red carpets in Hollywood. She pushed the food round her plate, thinking maybe she should hit the gym harder.

"What about… you know, skin?"

"*Skin?*"

"I'm not above that. I just want to get out there." She hated the ring of desperation she heard in her voice.

"T&A?" The agent gaped, unchewed food showing in her mouth. "Oh dear. You don't want tits and ass. You're better than T&A. You have a college degree, for God's sake."

"Don't tell me what I want."

She had the impression that someone was standing beside her. She looked up. It was the man who'd been making eyes at her from across the room. He was middle-aged, dressed untidily – his coat and sagging tweed pants had obvious tomato sauce stains – thin as a rail and sporting black-rimmed Coke-bottle glasses. His weak, watery blue eyes blinked slowly behind the thick lenses.

She perked up, passed her tongue over her teeth, in case there were lipstick stains, and smiled. She clicked through her mental Rolodex but didn't recognise him. Still, he could quite easily be someone influential in show business, a director, maybe. When he hesitated, she licked her lips, got the taste of gloss on them.

The man looked quizzically at her. Sticking out her chest, she sighed, held out a hand for a pen and paper.

"I'm sorry," the man said haltingly. "You seem, well, you look… Oh dear. I am sorry. I thought you were somebody."

She couldn't believe she was here. She looked around in awe, shivering slightly. The studio was freezing. She'd worn the wrong clothes, she realised in dismay – strappy spike heels and a frothy new gypsy dress that hung off her shoulders, beneath which she wore no underwear. But at least her new jewellery was blinging big-time. She'd maxed out her credit cards to deck herself out. Now she was broke. This was it. Her last shot at making the jump. She tried to ignore the ripple of cold that ran through her, hardening her nipples. She wasn't complaining, though; a nationally syndicated late-night talk-show had finally called.

The show's host had personally left her flowers, along with a polite handwritten note requesting that she join him in his dressing room after the show. For a blowjob? She made a mental note to get a commitment from him first; she'd been screwed over by too many people she'd given blowjobs and afterwards had nothing to show for it, except chocolates, a few pieces of jewellery and a pair of expensive shoes.

She thought about her idol, Mae West, and tried to channel her.

Interviewer: "Goodness, what jewellery!"

West (throwing back her head and laughing throatily): "Goodness had nothing to do with it, dearie!"

The show's production manager was a nervous little man with

headphones and a clipboard who'd been helpful in getting her situated. He poked his head around the dressing room door. "Knock, knock. Are we decent?" he asked.

She looked up, smiling crookedly.

"Comfy? Do you need anything at all? Good. Quick thing – you're up right after the break," he said, ignoring her fidgeting.

"Oh, I'm just nervous."

"C'mon! Just look at that face. You'll photograph well. Don't be nervous."

She checked her reflection in the mirror. "OK."

"By the way, big show tonight." Winking, he added, "Glenn Close. You're in good company."

Later, she wandered from the green room, waited in the wings and watched the show on a small monitor with the rest of the crew. She studied the star's relationship first with the cameras and then the audience, which was enthusiastic, eager to see a famous person. She shivered with cold, scanning the audience for potential talent scouts. Her feet hurt in her ridiculous shoes. She stepped out of them.

At the break, the producer came to tell her that her segment had been shifted down to the final quarter of the show. "Don't worry, hon," he said, giving her arm a reassuring little squeeze. "You'll get to tell your story."

She stared at his retreating figure, stricken. When she went back to the wings, the crew were talking.

"It's running overtime," someone said.

"The last segment might get canned."

"Might? Ten bucks says it's gonna, for sure."

"What's her story anyway?"

"Saved a kid from drowning. Some shit like that."

"Man, Glenn Close. Are you kidding me? Cruella Deville trumps kid-saving any day of the week."

There was a flurry of activity behind the scenes, with people scurrying all around her. She felt as if she were no longer present, as if she were eavesdropping on a private conversation not meant for her. She waited, the sinking feeling in her gut becoming stronger with each passing segment of the show.

Then it was over. Glenn Close had left and the show was over.

Connie stood shoeless, still in the wings, while the show's theme song played. "That's it, people!" someone shouted. "That's a wrap."

"Sorry, we ran out of time." The producer approached her, shrugging. He was nibbling on a Granny Smith apple. The action of his teeth, which were slightly big, reminded her of a bunny gnawing at a carrot. "That's show business for you. Sometimes things don't work out."

Then he was gone, and the crew was scampering about. She looked around. The host had finished shaking hands and signing autographs for the studio audience and was preparing to leave the room. She tried to catch his eye when he walked close by her. She smelt the musk of his aftershave and imagined what it would be like in his arms, beneath him in bed, the weight of his warm body gently crushing her. She angled close to him, touched his sleeve. She wanted to say, "Hi, it's me. You don't remember? You wrote me a nice note. You wanted to see me in your dressing room after the show."

But the words remained frozen on her lips when he turned and looked right through her.

MORTALS

The baby's cancer has come back.

Lisa watches the doctor's mouth forming words, which she doesn't hear, although she knows them all too well. It's like watching TV with the volume down, only there is sound, a blur of noise around him, the normal sounds of the ward. Lisa continues watching him, dazed, her mouth slack, as if she's in a dream. But it is no dream. After six months of cautious optimism and finally beginning to breathe again, Lisa feels a familiar weight settle in the pit of her stomach.

Then the volume seems to be turned up again and she can again distinguish his words, though not clearly, as if they are coming from some distant place.

"I'm sorry, Mrs Stanton. I know this is the last thing you wanted to hear. I mean, we knew the risks with AML. But, I guess one never is fully prepared for a relapse. Of course, we'll do everything to fight back – we'll use a new combination of drugs. And there's the clinical trial for that new chemo regimen I spoke to you and your husband about. The hope is for remission, so an allogeneic stem cell transplant can be performed. The outlook, as we've discussed before, is not the best. Whatever happens, though, you should know we're in for the long haul."

That's it, then. He is sorry. It's over? Lisa feels confused. What is he saying? She feels like a child, unable to comprehend, though she thinks she should, and decides not to ask him to explain. She feels exhausted. She wants to lie down somewhere, curl up and go to sleep.

Lisa is nearly always exhausted. She walks with a plodding gait and regularly emits weary sighs. Though she is still good-looking, thank God, when she looks at herself in the mirror, she says to her

16

reflection, "Who will love me again?", staring into eyes that are often bloodshot and have dark smudges beneath them. She keeps a tube of concealer in her medicine chest to cover the circles; it's the only make-up she ever uses now. Peering some more at the face, she made other unpleasant discoveries: her cheekbones seem too exaggerated, too pronounced for her now gaunt face, as though they belonged to someone else – perfect for some ano-rexic runway model but for her, they're too severe, making her look like a fierce-eyed savage. Worse was her discovery that her post-pregnancy body with its luscious, womanly curves – the full boobs, the accentuated hips – with which she'd fallen in love, and with which Steven had been enthralled, had all but disappeared. She's actually quite skinny now – emaciated even; she'd stopped eating again, and lost weight rapidly since the baby has taken a turn for the worse. For her visit to the hospital, she has brushed her hair back severely into a neat bun, from which not one loose strand of hair can escape. She is prophylactically dressed in a high-necked, ruffled pink Victorian blouse, a knee-length dun-col-oured pleated skirt whose waist is now too loose, and sensible tan pumps. She looks like a believer (which she isn't) in a particularly strict Christian sect, or perhaps an old-fashioned woman dressed for work at some government office. But Lisa no longer works; she quit her job after the baby's sickness reappeared.

She stands looking at the child almost serenely, and brushes her hand against the baby's feeble arm and offers it a small, placating smile before turning away from what she sees as a look of simultaneous hope and dismay clouding its eyes.

It's a setback, of course, the doctor continues, staring at the baby's chart – and avoiding looking at her, Lisa realises. Her mind wanders listlessly. His words sound almost like an admission – though of what, she is uncertain. It can't be of guilt. She's the guilty one, she's the one responsible for passing on this sickness from her womb.

The doctor is a slightly built, light-skinned man with a slight stoop, sloping shoulders and a smattering of freckles across his nose and cheeks. Lisa thinks it is funny for a black person, regardless of lightness of hue, to have freckles. Staring at his thinning widow's peak, she has a sudden urge to giggle. We're all going to die, she thinks, and the thought makes her queasy. Beads of sweat erupt on her forehead.

A fat nurse waddles by in her too-tight uniform, her pudgy, white-stockinged legs rubbing together noisily with a hissing sound. Lisa wonders if she plans to start a fire. Overweight, Lisa mentally corrects herself, that's the politically correct term. The nurse gives Lisa a tight, sympathetic smile, her chins wobbling, and Lisa, who is unable to look away from her, feels somehow exposed, diminished by this fat woman who perhaps has perfect – normal – children of her own.

To take her mind off these spiteful feelings brewing within her, Lisa focuses her attention on the doctor. He is reputedly one of the best paediatric oncologists in the Caribbean. She looks at his nameplate through a sudden blur of tears. Dr J Paul Mountbatten. Mountbatten. A regal name. Isn't the Queen a descendant of some Mountbattens or other? And what about his Christian name? Is the J for John? No, it wasn't something that common. She'd heard a doctor colleague of his, a well-preserved woman, maybe in her late-forties, greet him by his first name. Something Spanish? What was it? *I ought to know my child's doctor's first name*, she thinks angrily.

The doctor is still flipping through the baby's charts, as if for the answer to some unknown question. Lisa feels offended by this action. The tears that had been gathering in her eyes and in the back of her throat a moment ago have evaporated. *Look at me!* she wants to scream at him. *Why are you telling me this?*

In a corner of the ward, which is painted a soothing, neutral light yellow, a bald baby begins to wail. There is a movement towards the cot by the overweight nurse. Lisa looks at her with contempt.

Lisa's knees feel like rubber. She turns back to face the doctor and is struck by a wave of nausea. Hug me, she thinks wildly. Squeeze the loneliness out of me. She imagines herself collapsing helplessly in a sobbing ball at his feet. She would indeed launch herself at his feet, if that would help, if that would save her child's life.

His beeper goes off. He retrieves it from his waist and frowningly examines it before replacing it. He does not excuse himself, which is a relief for Lisa, who just now feels the need to be near him. As she watches him go over the chart she wants to throw herself at him, peel off his skin and burrow inside. But she will not embarrass herself; she will not embarrass him. Her own embarrassment is secondary, unimportant. She knows about other people's embarrassment; it is something she has become intimately acquainted with during the past few years. She is accustomed to the nervous titters of preschoolers, the shifty looks in their parents' eyes when they are out in public, in the waiting room at the doctor's, for example, when the baby is seized with nausea and starts projectile vomiting. "It's the chemo," Lisa would explain, compelled to apologise in her *forgive-me-for-all-this* tone of voice, the voice she had often used on her husband before he left. The parents would huddle their children close to them, nod uncomfortably, avoiding eye contact. As if they, too, thought it was all her fault that her child was sick and dying.

Outside the hospital it's a gloriously brilliant March day that makes the eyes hurt. After eleven successive days of rain the sky is clear and blue; everything is lush and green, cruelly alive; as if the greyness and death inside the building does not exist. Lisa breathes in deeply, looking up at the sun. Nobody tells you how hard it is being a single parent of a sick child. She even wishes that she had been raised with some faith so that she could pray. It feels like there's a conspiracy of silence about the difficulty, even among other parents of chronically and terminally-ill children. It was how it was with women who'd had children and were reluctant to tell the truth about the real pain of childbirth or that pregnancy often made a woman horny, endlessly dreaming of penises, penises and more penises.

She tries to throw up in a corner of the recently mown front lawn and when she is unable to do so, goes to sit on a concrete bench beneath an ancient lignum vitae tree; under it, mounds of raked leaves mixed in with mown grass and general trash and debris stand waiting to be bagged and tossed out. She stares at a bug marching up the side of the tree trunk, the dappled mid-morning sun's rays warm against her face. There are many benches like this one, scattered across the grounds. To help family members compose their thoughts about what faces their loved ones, she imagines. She notices a man and woman seated on a nearby bench beneath another tree. The man has his hand around the slender slumped shoulders of the woman who is staring blankly into space.

Lisa averts her eyes. She can hear the muffled sound of traffic in the distance, the world going on without a care for her problems. She thinks about her mother, who died in the first year she and Steven were married. Thinking about this is not a good idea. Never has she felt so much like an orphan. She has never been in touch with her father, who'd never taken an active role in her life. A divinity student from a prominent Westmoreland family, he'd had an affair with Lisa's mother for almost two years, then dumped her when Lisa was born. Her mother was the secretary at the Bible College where he'd been studying. His family's lawyers had discreetly arranged for a generous maintenance package for the child, with the stipulation that there would be no public identification of their bastard grandchild's father. Who was there to tell? Lisa's mother had no other living relatives. She found another secretarial job after she had the baby, and devoted herself to Lisa's welfare and happiness, raising her less like a daughter than a sister. They'd even double-dated a few times in Lisa's teenage years. Lisa's friends had all been amazed at the openness of their relationship, how they spoke honestly about sex, for instance. Because of her own bad experience, Lisa's mother urged her daughter to give her virginity only to a man who was worthy of her. Lisa *had* waited until she'd finished high school to engage in her first sexual encounter, though the man had undoubtedly not been worthy – his name had long escaped her – simply a man who'd offered her lift one rainy day as she stood waiting at a bus stop. Lisa, at eighteen, felt as though she hadn't completely disappointed her mother because she'd waited, and that had to count for something.

Now, Lisa feels the familiar dull ache in her breasts. She remembers how sharp the pain had been, the burning pain in both nipples, when she'd been nursing. How that electric suck of the baby's lips on the swollen tips, the lightning rod sensation zigzagging straight to her womb and oh, the delicious but illicit thrill of the pain, had made her feel more of a woman than at any other time in her life. How desperately she wishes she could still speak to her mother – the former festival queen who drew swarms of men buzzing like bees around flowers. She had been so young looking, and in seemingly good health, when a stroke felled her one morning and she'd died a week later. In retrospect, Lisa remembered the lingering flu that had developed into a bronchial infection. Lisa had been crippled by a sense of abandonment that whole first year of her marriage, leaning heavily on Steven for emotional support. For two weeks after the funeral she had stayed home in bed, too depressed to face the world, beseeching Steven to take time off work to stay at home with her. She had imagined her mother being around to enjoy the arrival of the grandchildren she'd anxiously anticipated from the day she'd walked Lisa down the aisle.

What comes after? Lisa asks herself now. "Let go, and let God," is the reply inside her head, which is really nothing but the echo of a non-sequitur she'd heard her father using to his well-heeled congregation, several times during one of his sermons. Lisa had kept close tabs on him and knew when he'd moved to Kingston to take up an appointment there. He'd become a respected and charismatic figure within ecumenical circles. Despite her bitterness at his treatment of her, she would sometimes creep into the back of the church to watch him. She was always struck by his handsomeness, his articulateness. He'd gone grey at the temples and some of his muscle tone had begun to go soft, but she could still divine the lover in him. She could understand how her mother had been seduced by him, by his silver tongue that she imagined had called on the name of Jesus even as he'd thrust, swollen and insistent, into her mother's yielding flesh. The truth was, as she glanced round at the adoring faces of his female congregants, who hung on to his every word, throwing their amens and hallelujahs wantonly at him as though they were undergarments, she was secretly a little proud of him. That day, as the organ swelled mournfully in the background, Lisa had watched him in his sober suit and formal tie, his secret life locked within his breast. "When nothing's left," he had intoned – a flash of a bracelet appearing from beneath his cuff when he held up a forefinger in admonition – "Friends, God is there."

But he isn't really, she thinks now. Faith was what people leaned on to get them through difficult times, but she can't bring herself to start believing in a god she despises, one of whose representatives was a hypocrite like her father. Still, where did it leave her as far as her understanding of the end of life? It's an issue she's been thinking about more and more. You go through all that shit, that pain and suffering in life and then, at the end, what is there? More pain and suffering? There was no guarantee of heaven, especially for someone who did not believe there was such a place. But, if not heaven, what?

She closes her eyes and tries to summon the presence of this god of whom her father spoke. But she can't. That god doesn't exist. The baby will return to the dust, that's all. So will she, when it's her turn to go. Nothing comes after. All that she can believe in is what's real, what came before, what is here and now. But wallowing in the morbid does no good, so she forces herself to think about other matters. Eyes still closed, she tries to reconstruct images of what her life had been before the baby. She'd been reasonably happy despite the less-than-perfect circumstances of her childhood. She'd grown up and had friends and she'd even known love. When she'd gotten pregnant, she'd felt her life was complete, especially because she'd believed that having children would be impossible. The baby. What joy she'd felt on her safe arrival. This perfect creature. Ten fingers, ten toes. All functioning parts. She was in love, again. There had been no thought, in those early days and nights when she cradled her to her bosom and gazed lovingly into her eyes, that she was one of those defective models that ought to be returned to the manufacturer. It hadn't occurred to her that there could be a problem.

Then, as the days turned into weeks, irritability, melancholy and restlessness had crept in. She felt guilty, as though she'd fallen out of love with the baby. Postpartum depression, the doctor had diagnosed. She didn't exactly ignore the baby, but she was no longer as fascinated with her every move. It was during this time that she also began to sense that things with Steven had hit some kind of snag. Her doctor encouraged her to return to work, and she did. Now, she cannot really remember what her days were like when she had a computer on her desk and wore daring high heels with professional cotton-blend suits that her boss and co-workers admired.

She will have to dismantle the baby's room, the room she'd spent so much time preparing. The furniture will have to be put in storage. Then there are all the cute little clothes to sort: she'll give some to Joan from the office, who recently had a baby; the others she'll give to goodwill –

Horrified, she realises that she's already begun to think about the baby as dead; she forces herself to stop.

She pulls out her cellphone and dials her husband. He left her and their child because he couldn't "stand the smell of sickness" and the way it made her so "damn needy".

"Yes, Lisa," Steven answers wearily, on the fourth ring, just before voice-mail chips in.

"Steven," she says without preamble. She pictures him, slight and effete, fragile as a baby bird. Neat, well-groomed. Dressed in a pin-striped suit, the jacket close-fitting, double-buttoned. People called his look metrosexual, he'd once told her, and she'd had to stifle the snigger that wanted to burst from her throat. "It's back." She thinks of their days at Lamaze classes, and pictures Steven holding her hand in the delivery room. They were once best friends. When had they become enemies? She listens to him breathing noisily through his mouth on the other end of the line. Adenoids.

"What? What's back?

"It's the baby," Lisa explains. "It's back."

There is silence. Then: "Jesus Christ." He expels a long frustrated sigh, and she can imagine him rubbing the elegant high bridge of his nose. "Where are you? Well, look, I'm in the middle of something here," he says. "I have to call you back. This evening, OK?"

She hangs up before he does, knowing what he's thinking. He's thinking she is using the baby's sickness as leverage to get him to come back home. There is a hurricane of emotions swirling around inside her, feelings she is unable to express. She doesn't want him back, and yet she does; she can't go through this alone. Mostly, though, she's confused; the idea that *he* would ever have left had never occurred to her.

She gets up and wanders back towards the building, but at the sliding glass door, changes her mind. The thought of going back inside there with the sickening hospital smell of antiseptic makes her want to retch again, and so urgent does the need to pee become, that she hurries around the side of the building instead.

The hospital's grounds are huge. She remembers seeing them first on a brochure someone from her workplace had handed her. She remembers thinking that surely the baby would be cured at such an impressive structure as this. The hospital itself is a magnificent ivory-coloured edifice with sloping green-shingled roofs. It had been built in the economic boom of the mid-1980s, by the government with assistance from the Jewish business-men's league. Lisa's footfalls are soundless in the high grass around the side of the building.

Lisa vomits, then squats to pee when she finds a suitable spot, near a pile of leaves under a tree. A sound somewhere makes her pause, mid-flow, a Kegel contraction that makes her pubis throb with pleasure. She looks up and sees that she is being observed by the grounds-keeper, a stocky deaf-mute she's seen around the institution. He also works as a cleaner on the wards; Lisa remem-bers seeing him with his mops and other accoutrements. They had on occasion exchanged looks; there was one time Lisa noticed something in his eyes. Steven had noticed it too. They had been on the ward one night, when he'd come up the hall, noisily dragging his roller bucket with the squeaky wheels, dirty water sloshing out over the sides. The baby had just been diagnosed; they'd been keeping vigil beside her cot.

Lisa had looked up and had seen him in the hallway, staring at her, his mouth half-open in his deaf-mute gape. She could tell then, simply by looking at him, that something was wrong with him. Lisa knew it was impolite to stare but she was unable to drag her eyes away. Perhaps because of what had befallen them, she couldn't help finding something morbidly compelling in sick-ness and disability. Their eyes held for a few seconds before Steven put a protective arm around her. "Is it safe to have that guy here, on the ward with the children?" he had whispered when the cleaner had moved down the hall. "He's kind of creepy."

Lisa looks at the deaf-mute now and realises that she cannot estimate his age – it could be anywhere between late teens and thirties. He is dressed in khaki and water boots and carries a coiled-up garden hose. His fleshy lips are hanging open, the way they had been when she'd first seen him on the ward. She wonders if he remembers her. Probably not. Possibly he's re-tarded as well. No sooner is the thought out than she feels ashamed for thinking it. Her mind runs back to the nurse she'd judged as fat. When did she become so mean?

She is frightened by a sound he makes in his throat.

"Oh," Lisa says, and, filled with a reckless daring, empties the rest of her bladder.

He mutters something unintelligible and backs away.

Lisa knows what an incongruous picture she must have made with her serious hairstyle and dignified clothes, the sensible pleated skirt hiked up above her knees, squatting down above the high, vomit-sprayed grass like a Vietnamese peasant, the gusset of her pants pulled aside by her finger, pee splashing against the sides of her tan shoes. But in that instant, she doesn't care. Her pants have gotten wet, too, so she pulls them down, wads them up and stuffs them into her handbag. He probably hasn't taken in any of it, she tells herself. She takes out a square of Kleenex from the mini pack she keeps handy in her purse, and dabs at herself before reaching down to dab at the leather of her shoes splashed by urine. "God," she says aloud. She tosses away the tissue, looks around. "God," she says again.

When she finds him he is attaching the hose to a standpipe. From where she stands she can smell the rank odour of sweat in his clothes.

She approaches, her heart beating erratically. She feels awk-ward, as if she is just learning to walk; it has been a while since she seduced anyone. She must tread carefully, she cannot spook him. Above, a bird alights from a tree, wings flapping, startling her.

She stops.

He stops dead, too, looks up, slack-jawed. She smiles at him. She has not been with a man in more than a year; her smile is meant to inspire desire, despite the awkward circumstances. She hopes it does. Unable to stop herself now, she hikes up her skirt – what *is* she doing? – revealing her crotch with its untamed bush.

She hears the same strangled sound come from him, and her eyes travel boldly to the front of his pants, which she sees has formed an appreciative tent. She is glad he is unable to speak. Glad that in spite of this, he can nevertheless be made to understand.

She is down on all fours – her dun-coloured pleated skirt bunched up around her waist. He kneels behind her. Nothing matters now – not her dead mother, the infant lying inside the sick children's ward, the goddamned husband who puked the first time he smelt the baby's puke, and then moved out, not the fact that she has no money left for this go-round of hospital fees and medication and whatnot – nothing matters except that there is a strange man inside her, and all she can feel inside her is him.

But this isn't quite enough. She pulls away from him, and pushes him down on his back and straddles him, impaling herself on his rigid cock. His shirt is ringed with the sweat stains of one who labours for many hours beneath the sun; she peels it off and flings it as far away from them as she can. He is young, she decides – twenties, maybe – solid. She can see now that what she thought flab is actually muscle. His eyes are glazed with excitement and fear; his slack mouth reveals crooked yellowed teeth.

Her face feels flushed, an angry vein appearing in the centre of her forehead; her nostrils are flaring. She feels good, in charge of her circumstances, for once. The feeling of power is almost more than she can bear. It's better than thinking of the unfairness of it, belonging to a god she can't see or believe in. As if from a distance, she can hear the sound of their laboured breathing – grunts and groans – and a voice urging, *Faster, faster, faster, faster* that she does not recognise.

After, she vomits again. Then she adjusts her hair, and examines her knees where the earth has bruised them. She looks at him, the deaf-mute, dazed, his pants bundled around his ankles, and sees it had been a new and not unpleasant experience for him. She imagines him thinking about her later that night in his bed, and knows she will absolutely not want him again. This episode will remain a secret.

Secrets.

Lisa knows all about secrets, and how to keep them. She has never told a soul – except, of course, Steven – who her father is. It would be a colossal embarrassment to him, his family – perhaps cost him his church if she were to decide to come forward now. She remembers once fantasising about it and telling Steven, "Maybe I should just stand up one day and tell everybody that he's my father." They'd been lying on their big comfortable leather sofa one Sunday evening while they watched TV.

She'd returned earlier that afternoon from one of her visits to his church, which had been more frequent after her mother died. As usual, Steven had prepared dinner, Italian fare, and they'd eaten and gone to the living room to watch a movie. She was still in her stockings and frowned when Steven took one of her feet gently into his lap and started massaging it with his soft, pampered hands. Lisa told him how her father had bragged to his congregants that his son, his "firstborn", had been accepted into a foreign Bible school and would soon join him in the ministry. "I should have just stood up, made a scene. Told everybody that I'm his firstborn," Lisa said, quite taken aback by the venom she was feeling.

"Are you crazy?" Steven had asked sharply.

Lisa had assured him it was only a joke; she had no interest in ruining the man's life. But Steven had stopped rubbing her feet and turned his attention to the TV. Secrets were important to him, too, particularly the sanctity of keeping them. He himself had a secret: a big one. When they'd agreed to marry, it entailed acceptance of the regular late-night sounds of male laughter seeping through his adjacent bedroom wall, for example. For her, it was a small price to pay to allay the fear of becoming a lonely, childless old maid. He'd entrusted her with custodianship of his secret, depending on her to guard it with her life.

To this day, she had.

She re-emerges from under the tree into the brilliance of the day, the pulse in her throat throbbing like an explosive device on the brink of detonation. The day has begun to heat up, she notes, glancing down at her blouse moist with perspiration. Beneath the fabric of her skirt, her nakedness feels exquisite. It reminds her of the days when she was desirable, when she had lovers – married ones, and single ones. She would call them, teasing that she was naked beneath her clothes and she was touching herself, thinking about them. She pauses to steady herself, her secret furled deep within her like a prayer. Yes, she knows how to keep secrets.

At the sliding glass door entrance, she bumps into the baby's doctor.

"Mrs Stanton," he says, a concerned frown creasing his brow. "We were wondering where you'd got to. Are you all right?"

"Yes. I'm fine, Doctor. I just needed, I needed some fresh air."

"Oh. Well, let's go up to see your daughter." He touches her arm lightly, propels her through the lobby, which is bright with crystal sunshine, oversized potted plants and a shiny marble floor, to the elevator that will take them up to the children's ward.

As they stand side by side, quietly staring up at the lighted buttons that signal which floor the lift has reached, Lisa suddenly remembers what the J stands for, and this recollection of the elusive Christian name brings her more satisfaction than anything else that has happened to her in a long while. She repeats the name in her head like a mantra. For a moment she is invincible. She closes her eyes and sighs deeply, breathing the name softly on her lips. She can feel the doctor standing there beside her. All around her, she is aware of people rushing about, the sick and the un-sick – mortals – their murmured words rising up like some strange and wonderful force field.

LAPDANCE

It's like some weird mating dance going on between me and this girl who's standing before me, taking her clothes off. We're inside this strip club called Pussycats, a dive on a seamy little street in the Village cluttered with beauty supplies stores, speciality sex shops, delis, dirty bodegas and shambling grey buildings that at night host wild rave parties, crawling with club rats wearing expensive eyeliner, trannies in fake Prada and Gucci trying to hustle $5-hand jobs on the corner, crack whores wanting like hell to hit the pipe, and whacked-out bums jonesing for the next drink. It's a grim night, the way Village nights can be, with the smell of piss, degradation and fucked-up dreams leaching out of the walls of every old building. Heaven on frigging earth, right? Sometimes I wonder what the hell am I doing here.

I'm here because I love lapdances. They're my poison. Chillin' in the champagne room, son. I figure people would say I'm addicted to them. That's a hell of a thing to get addicted to. But what can I tell you? I'm here three, four times a week. Reckon that's better than hitting the crack pipe. And let me tell you, there's lots of reasons why I could go there. But that's another story.

So I'm in Pussycats. Ha. Like, I'm so into pussies, you wouldn't understand. Gettin' jiggy with it, like my man Will Smith said. And so there's this new chickie, right? Not one of the regulars. Usually I get Cheyenne or Lotsa Lovin' or Freedom Chains. Those girls know me, know what I like and ain't got no problems giving it to me. I don't have to draw them a picture, if you get my meaning. I've been coming here for what, two years now. And, on account of the fact that they know I'm cool, I even get to touch them. You can never really tell the freaks just by looking, I guess.

But I ain't no freak. They know this, and that's how come they let me get close.

So. This new chick, Ambrosia. She's my dancer for tonight, right? I grin at her so she'll know I'm a nice guy. Nice name, I say. Do you know it means "food of the gods"?

She smiles and nods. I like that. Makes me feel good, you know. She's probably heard that same lame line hundreds of times from smartasses like me but she just acted like it was the first time. She's got this thing about her, this *sexycool* vibe, that just kills me. Hell, I ain't no poet, but it's like this quiet shyness or something. And then it strikes me: the thing that's different about this chick is that she doesn't act like she's just a slut. Like them other cock teases. Maybe she's new at this gig, but you can see right away that she takes pride in her job. In a weird way, this really turns me on.

She loosens my tie, unbuttons my shirtsleeves. I'm thinking if this was one of those *Leave it to Beaver*-type TV shows, maybe she'd get my slippers and a newspaper too. This is new, but I'm liking the fact that she's treating me like a human being and not like some john who's paying her for favours.

Then she starts to dance to a slow groove. I'm nursing a scotch-and-soda and feeling mellow as hell. She puts her little finger in her mouth and sucks it while she's swinging her hips. She's little in a black full-slip, not curvy and big-boned like the other girls. Her jet-black hair is short, pixyish. Like a boy's. Normally I like long hair on a woman. You fuck a woman with short hair and it's like you're fucking a guy, right? Hell, I'll say it again – I ain't no kind of queer. No sir. It's just, on this chick, the short hair is working.

She has on garters, mesh stockings and high heels. I can see her tits when she steps out of her shoes and leans forward to peel off the garters and stockings. They aren't very big. But I can tell they're firm – a neat little handful. I prefer big tits, but this is cool, too. This girl has no markings like the other girls: no tats, no piercings, nothing. At least, nothing I can see. Usually, I like tats on a girl. It makes them look like bad asses, especially when they're all curvy and shit. But this girl, well, she's as pure as the driven snow. And all the while I'm watching her, thinking how she isn't really my type, but swear to God, the bitch is making me feel so horny. Then slowly, slowly, she comes up to me kicking out her long legs like she's a cancan girl. Her black eyes are trained on me, deep and penetrating.

So now she's standing directly before me. Her little pink tongue slides out over her bottom lip. It's almost like she's moving in slow motion when she puts up one of her legs and swings it over mine. Then she puts it back down again and smiles at me. I don't have the patience for this shit.

I have this friend, a Yank named Charlie, who tells me that I'm a woman-hater. That's bullshit because I really dig chicks. Charlie's this pussified dude who believes in "being in touch with his feminine side". New Age psychobabble. I mean, the guy thinks that by being a punk, he's somehow better than me. Man, that limp-dick loser's my age and he's already engaged to this hot-shit fashion model piece of ass who I know is stepping out on him. He's always asking me why I don't have any women friends, why I screw every woman I know. Poor Charlie in his faggotty little Brooks' Brothers suits and his Bruno Maglis. He'll never understand why I'm the fucking man.

Hell, if I even understand it myself.

Anyway, so this Ambrosia chick starts straddling me, and I can smell her sweet girly smell, and next thing I know, I stop being mad with her. Man, I start getting so hot for her I think I'm going out of my mind. Swear to God, I almost blow my fuse right then and there. This Ambrosia's looking at me with her dark eyes that are telling me a thousand ways that I can violate her and all I know is that the blood starts swooshing from my head, loud like a runaway train.

Don't ask me why, but all I can do to hold on is to think about my first real girl friend, Yvette. Pronounced like *you-vette*. Ha, ha. You bet Yvette. Skinny Yvette from New York. Only skinny girl I ever been with. Yvette, with the tramp stamp of a black dick that came just over her G-string.

The first time I saw Yvette was a few years ago, at a park, at the annual company picnic. I'd just started working at Morrison and Findlay, a debt financing company in Manhattan. I'd recently left Georgia, where my moms and I had first migrated to from

Jamaica, and was new in town. It was my first job after college, entry-level y'know, no big thing, but I ain't ashamed to say I saw myself moving up the totem pole real quick.

Then I met Yvette, the boss's daughter. She looked like goddamned jailbait with her short-ass little pleated skirt, bobby socks and sneakers and blond hair tied in a ponytail. The girl was a walking wet dream, all bubblegum pink lips and creamy skin. A regular little pom-pom type like you see in nudie magazines frolicking butt-ass naked with a bunch of other co-eds all up for some hot lesbo action. Man, I was scared she'd get me fired. I'd been in this country long enough – I knew how it could chew up and spit out guys like me. I tried not to make eye contact with her, but it was damn hard. I could tell she seen me. The couple of times I let my gaze go over to her, she was staring at me. I knew she was the kind of girl that always fantasized about black guys, though she probably hadn't had any as yet.

She made the first move. She came over to me and pretty much let me know she was up for anything.

It was a warm first day of spring. All around us, families were out and about, spreading picnic tablecloths, tossing footballs, doing all the cornball stuff white folks do after a long bitter winter had turned their brains to mush. Overhead, the sky was blue and clear. A small wind whipped through the dogwood trees that grew up all graceful like around the park, circulating the smell of hot dogs and barbecued chicken, and my favourite: sweet potato pie.

I was sitting in a corner by myself, watching some of the guys from my office playing scrimmage a ways away. I didn't mind kicking around a ball but I wasn't part of the game because, as I said, I didn't know anybody yet. Yvette walked over to me and scooped up some potato salad from off my plate with her finger. Just like that. Then she put it in my mouth. "Lick it," she said, and I swear to Christ I almost came right there. After the picnic, I went home with her to her apartment. I stayed there all weekend.

Thinking about Yvette gets me excited all over again, right? So now I'm watching this Ambrosia chick. And I'm thinking that maybe she'll come home with me. I mean, what the hey? Ain't no *thang* but a chicken wing, you know what I'm sayin'. I've got an erection I don't wanna waste. It's been a while since I've had a woman in my bed; maybe this girl can warm my sheets. Why not? I'm a nice guy. Plus, it's payday. I've got money to burn. I pay for the champagne and I guess I kind of forget that she's new and doesn't know that some of the chicks don't bother with the "no-touching" policy when they're with me. I'm thinking that maybe I'll sample the goods before I proposition her, but when I grab her and try to push my finger inside her, two things happen. One: my fingers meet something lumpy – where there shouldn't be... Two: Ambrosia lets out this hellcat scream that scares the snot out of me. *What the hell*?

I'm just trying to get my bearings from the shock, so I'm disoriented and slow. When her hand comes up to belt me one in the face, I'm caught off guard.

She jumps off me and is screaming for the muscle in this weird male voice. It dawns on me that she hadn't spoken a word to me all along. Hands! Hands! she's going, like some freaked-out retard, clutching her chest and trembling.

That's when I notice the faint shadow of an Adam's apple bobbing up and down in her throat. Ambrosia with the Adam's apple. Did I notice it before, when I got hard for him? I think maybe I did. How could I not?

Shee-it.

Then the door bursts open and the Cavalry rushes in; the muscle named Smitty. What the hell is going on here? he shouts, rushing in, looking from me to her.

He is a bald-headed black guy, huge like CJ Hunter, only three times huger and definitely meaner-looking. He looks like he bench-presses guys like me every day. He's gripping a half-eaten burger in one hand, with a glob of mayonnaise at the corner of his fleshy mouth. There is a smudge of ketchup on his T-shirt, which has the word FCUK printed on it, is way too tight – stretched across his chest looking like it's on life support. I almost laugh at how ridiculous he looks.

Smitty belches and the sound and stinky smell filter across the room. Right away I know he's got some serious gastro-intestinal problems. He's a fucking slob, if you want to know. Even so, you didn't want to mess with a guy like Smitty. I sure as hell don't want to and I'm a big enough guy myself. Well, maybe not exactly big but, you know, I hold my own. But what Smitty had on me was density. Smitty was short and squat and looked like a mass of something – I don't know. A train wreck, perhaps.

What the hell's going on? he repeats, the burger shaking in his giant paw.

Chill the fuck out, *bro*.

But this Ambrosia chick is crying now and goes and stands behind him. He touched me, she says in her weird man-woman voice, pointing shakily at me.

Yeah I touched it. Sue me! I shout. But inside I'm Jell-O. I'm thinking, Man, I so don't want to get into it with Smitty.

Smitty looks at me, still clutching his burger, like he thinks someone's going to snatch it away from him. I can see he doesn't want to fight me. "Hey Jimmy," he says quietly, taking a step toward me.

"Hey. Ain't no thang but a chicken wing," I tell him, putting up my hands in surrender, and feeling my gut twist.

He keeps moving towards me, pointing to the sign on the wall: NO PHYSICAL CONTACT. "You know the rules, man. No touching. You don't touch the girls."

By this time, some of the other girls have heard the commotion and are crowding in at the door, looking in and whispering, though I can't quite catch what they're saying. I want to shout at them, I don't know, I guess I want them on my side. But at the same time I don't want to rat them out and get them in trouble by letting on that they make me touch them, so I don't say anything about that.

So I turn back to Smitty and say, Yeah, but you guys are taking my money under false pretences here. I paid for a dance with a woman. Instead, I get some sick *Crying Game* shit up in here!

What you talking 'bout, homes? Smitty goes, looking suspiciously at Ambrosia. What he do to ya, baby?

Sh-*it*. Are you fucking kidding me? This Ambrosia is a closet queen and nobody knows! Just look under her dress! I'm getting *really* pissed off now.

Meanwhile Ambrosia is hysterical. I mean there's waterworks all over the place. Her mascara's running down her cheeks and the dumb bitch even has a snot bubble in her nose and everything.

I look at her, and she looks back at me like she just found out I killed her cat. Like I'm the one that let her down. She's a real small dude, with small hands and wrists, and I see how easy she can pass for a dame.

All this time Smitty's watching us. He's looking from me to her like a big dumb dog. Like he ain't know what to do. Meanwhile, the tension in the room is thick, like you could cut it with a knife.

Then this Ambrosia starts wringing her hands and talking about how she's doing this so she can save towards getting the other part of her operation. Her eyes are all wild and I can see that she's scared. But all I want to do is beat the hell out of her. I want to beat her to a bloody pulp. I could just take her little body and crush it with my bare hands, squeeze her throat till I see her eyes roll over in her head. And I feel myself getting hard again, and all of a sudden I feel blind white rage and see Sonny inside my head, laughing at me and telling me I'm a queer.

Oh hell, no.

And I'm thinking, *I'm no faggot, man. I ain't no fucking faggot.*

That's when all hell breaks loose. I slip past Smitty and lunge for Ambrosia. Smitty grabs my hand and I think he's breaking all the bones in it. He twists it behind my back. Ambrosia takes the opportunity to make a dive for the doorway, bawling like a banshee. Then the girls start running all over the place. It's like this really bad scene from a western, like a salon brawl gone bad.

Then something kind of snaps inside me. I don't know, I twist out of Smitty's grasp and take a bite out of his hand. Just like that. Like it's a big old hand sandwich. His burger drops on the ground and I feel a tooth loosen; it's a big bite. Then I take a swing at him.

Sh-*it*.

Man, that's how it is with me sometimes. I don't think things all the way through. The minute I take that swing, I know I've made a mistake. His face gets kind of purple and his cheeks puff out and he makes this noise, like a tiger growling. I try to make a dash for the door but I'm too slow. Smitty charges after me, swearing and telling me I'm dead. He head-butts me and I feel like all the lights go off or I've gone blind and my lip feels split. Then next thing I know, Smitty is lifting me up off my feet, holding me by my nuts, and next thing I know is I'm propellering around in the air above his head and he's charging like a madman towards the back door.

The last thing I remember is sailing through the air before my skull connects with concrete.

Then it's nothing.

Uncle Sonny is looking down at me lying there on my back, and laughing. I haven't thought about him in, like, a lifetime. But it's the same old Sonny. His front tooth has the same chip from the time we fell out of a tree at the back of my grandmother's house. I know it's a dream, even though it seems real 'cause Sonny and me are kids again. He's twelve and I'm eight. We're like cousins, being so close in age and all. Like brothers.

So, Sonny and me are here in this whacked-out concussed state. We're on the roof of my grandmother's house, a little one-room in a fucked-up part of town with a view of the city dump. When my old man ran out on my moms shortly after I was born, we moved in with her. That place could rival any of the projects and slums I've seen here in the States. All I know is once we got out on a plane and got the hell out of there we didn't look back.

Those were shitty days. Then my moms met the American and married him to get the green card. It was a long time ago but every now and again I think about those days before we left. I don't remember a whole lot. I was young, just a kid. But I can't ever forget that house. It was real tiny, too. Even though there were only a few pieces of furniture – a pea-green couch that was split, with the stuffing overflowing, and a fold-up dining-room table, a small fridge and a gas range – it always felt cluttered.

We used to love going up on my grandma's roof, Sonny and me, especially at night. The house had a slab roof so it got real hot real quick. We'd go up there with the hose and wet down the roof. Then we'd just sit there in our pyjamas feeling the air on our faces and listen to crickets and croaking lizards and shit and watch the smoke hovering like a film over the dump.

Sonny didn't have any friends. On account of him being funny in the head, I guess. People said it was because my grandmother had him too late in life. He was almost twenty years younger than my moms. They said he was a retard. But he wasn't. He used to like that folks thought he was an idiot. It was weird, but he did. I guess he wanted to be able to get away with stuff.

So anyway, in the nights, Sonny and me would be up there on the roof, pretending we were kings and the stars in the sky were our kingdoms, our royal subjects, like in the storybooks. Whatever. I would always try to count them, the stars. Sonny would tell me that we couldn't, then I'd bet him he could. We'd start off real good though, 'til Sonny started calling out arbitrary numbers to trip me up, so I'd get confused and forget where I'd reached. Then we would sort of just fall back and laugh like we were big old fools. Sonny was all right, man. He was goofy, but he was all right.

So in the dream we're in our pyjama bottoms on the roof like we always were. Then the weird shit happens. It's like some freaky déjà-vu thing and I'm living out something that feels like it happened to me before. In the distance, smoke from the city dump is trailing up into the sky. We start counting stars. All I know is I'm counting stars and Sonny's calling out mixed-up random numbers trying to confuse me.

Stop, Sonny, I say and laugh.

But he doesn't stop. No, sir. He just keeps on shouting out numbers while I'm counting. Then he leans over and starts tickling me. We start rolling around on the roof, shrieking with laughter. Sonny's tickling me so much I think I'm going to piss myself. But it feels good, that feeling that you get when somebody's tickling you and you want them to stop and at the same time you kind of don't.

Next thing is he's touching me. And he wasn't so all right any more. I don't like it, I swear to God. I feel myself getting hard. It feels weird. Like something that's not supposed to happen. Mama says no one's s'posed to touch me, Sonny, I say, feeling my mouth fill up with something bitter. I tell him. I tell him that. I tell him no, I know I do. But he only laughs.

Oh, you just a baby, he says. His eyes are mean, meanest eyes I ever seen him with. Then he starts mimicking me. Mama says no one's supposed to touch me down there, Sonny. I feel like shit. The way I do when he double dares me to crawl over the

Grahams' front gate at midnight and raid their mango tree and I know I can't because I'm scared.

Cry-cry baby, he mocks.

I'm not a baby, I say. Take it back.

Make me, Sonny says and shoves me. I can hear crickets chirping around us in the dark. Feel the hair on the back of my neck standing up. Then I start to cry 'cause I hate it when Sonny doesn't love me. When Mama goes to work at night he stays with me. Sometimes he lets me play with his toy cars. I like that. I don't want him to get mad at me.

So I say, OK. I feel relieved when he smiles. I let go and relax, and it feels good, his mouth on me. And I know it's wrong but I don't know how to not make it feel so right.

Now it's your turn, he says when he's through. He tugs on his zipper. It makes a quick metallic sound in the dark.

When it's over he whispers, Good boy. You cain't tell a soul, OK? Swear.

I swear, and because we're brothers I never tell a soul.

The next thing I know is I'm waking up in the alley in the back of the club, with blood coming from my mouth, a couple teeth loose, and a gash somewhere on my forehead. There's the stink of some nearby dumpsters. The temperature has fallen a couple of degrees and it's chilly. I look down at myself and see that I'm still in my jacket but my tie's missing. I'm lying in a heap; one of my legs is twisted in a kind of right angle and hurting like a son of a bitch so I know it's probably broken. I can't move so I can't look at my watch, but it feels late, like maybe one, two in the morning.

There is a sudden movement somewhere in the distance and my heart starts to beat fast. I hold my breath. Maybe Smitty's coming back. But it's only a cat, scrounging around, sniffing an old take-out food box. It jumps down, then stops frozen in its tracks to inspect me. In the darkness its animal eyes look like glass.

I try to sit up but I can't move. Smitty really tap-danced all over my ass, but all I can think about is how everything's going to change after tonight. And I'm struggling, struggling – going under, man. The smell of rotting food from the nearest dumpster gets in my nose, in my throat. I swear to Christ I want to gag. I think about the guys I know. Well, Charlie, really, since I don't have a hell of a lot of friends who are dudes. Have I ever got wood thinking about him before? I don't think so. But how the fuck can I be sure?

The cat mews, still staring at me. It doesn't even consider running away, that's how much of a joke I guess I seem to it lying there like that. Shoo, I hiss at it, wishing I could get my fingers around its neck. It scampers off and I close my eyes and settle back against the hard, cold concrete.

I start thinking about everything that happened earlier that night. My skin begins to crawl even as I begin to feel the rumblings of a cock-stand while conjuring up Ambrosia's face. What am I? I'm a joke. Everything in my life has been a joke. One big friggin' lie. The women, everything. Mr Lover Man. What a big fraud.

I don't know how long I stay like that; it could be hours, it could be minutes. I don't know. There's this long, dreamlike feel to the night, see? But time don't seem all that important now. Besides, I've got this feeling I'm gonna have nothing but time on my hands from here on out. Nothing but time. And I don't do a thing. I don't do a damn thing but sit there, in that alley, breathing in all that rot, that stink from the dumpsters, and I can't move, I can't do anything because, what the hell? Nothing's gonna be the same again.

PRIVATE LIVES OF GIRLS AND WOMEN

My daughter is pregnant. The news couldn't have come at a more inopportune time. At least – and I know this will seem self-indulgent – it is inopportune for me. She, however, is ecstatic. She is sixteen, and she trumpets the news of her imminent motherhood at the family Christmas dinner, as if she's a network TV news anchor, smiling broadly at us, her captive audience – we parents, her idiot boyfriend, her younger brother and her grand-parents. As if it is a perfectly natural and acceptable state for her to be in. She wants to pack her things and get the hell out of my house so she can be on her own, experience "real life", as she puts it. She is glowing.

Looking at her dreamy expression, her dewy, lopsided grin, I am filled with murderous rage. I want to tell everybody to go. I need to be left alone.

I hate Christmas. It's the time of year when I have to play the roles of daughter and mother simultaneously; I'm not good at either. A person should be one or the other, not both. It's been a relentlessly dismal day, too, with rain falling in fits and starts across the city. By dinner, though the sun was peeping out weakly from between grey-bellied clouds, rainwater was still gushing down the gutters lining the street. With this atmosphere of gloom, I should have guessed that things would take a sharp downward spiral. How could I not have seen it coming?

The living room smells of the pine needles already shedding from the Christmas tree. We chit-chat before sitting at the table, exchange hugs and double-cheek kisses. I'm a bundle of nerve endings – maybe my body's way of alerting me there's trouble ahead.

On the component set, Kenny G's *O Holy Night* is playing softly. The table is spread with chicken, ham, rice and peas and sorrel. At the place settings, the silverware is understated, unpretentious.

"Well, everything seems quite nice, dear," says my mother, in a forced-happy voice that says it's not. My mother likes frills and flounces. "Very utilitarian," she observes drily. *Thanks, Mom,* I think. *I do so enjoy a little condescension with my dinner.* My parents, who now reside in Canada, are home for the holidays, and are staying with us this year instead of with my older sister, Yvonne (Mom's favourite), and her family, who are spending Christmas this year in Kentucky with Yvonne's American husband's folks. My mother looks around and smiles another of her tight smiles that do not show her teeth. Diamonds glint in her ear lobes. "Of course, Yvonne would have done a bigger spread. But then, her table's twice as big, I suppose."

I am, I think, on the brink of a nervous breakdown.

After the blessing of the food, which Gareth, my husband, delivers, I look across the table and try to coax out a feeling of gratitude. We are together for another year and for this I should be happy. But I am not. Jennifer, my best friend, has lost both her parents this past year to cancer and, as if that wasn't bad enough, found out that her husband has been having an affair and is planning to leave her and their children. I'm lucky, I know. But I don't *feel* lucky. Holidays and big family occasions always make me tense – the stress of getting everything perfect. On the night before my wedding, for example, I sat out on my parents' front lawn with what must have been the worst eczema outbreak in modern medical history, sobbing for about an hour, telling everyone I couldn't go ahead with the ceremony. Six months of meticulous planning had brought me to the edge of hysteria. I had to be put down with some Valium and a couple shots of my father's good brandy.

Before my daughter's baby news is delivered, my husband stands to get a comfortable line on the carving of the ham, which I know is badly overdone. He sniffs and says, "Mmm-hmm", enthusiastically bobbing his head. "Everything smells good." He is a liar, my big, wonderful liar, and I love him. I know he's trying to help; he knows that I am the worst cook ever. In fact, he'd suggested, as he does every time I have to cook a family meal, that

I get help. "Three words, sweetness," he'd said huffily, a few nights ago when I'd spurned his advances because I can't have sex when I'm stressed. "Call. A. Caterer."

I smile in spite of everything and nudge him under the table. I look across the table and see my daughter and her boyfriend exchanging significant looks and suppressing giggles. I can sense, with a mother's intuition, something is brewing between them. Bristling with conspiracy, as it turns out. When my daughter was little, I understood every unspoken thought she had. We'd always been so in tune with each other I'd assumed we'd be close even when she became a teen. These days, I look at her and am clueless about what is floating around inside her head, but with her eye-rolling and sighs of impatience, I suspect she's saying I'm the adversary of her soul.

Staring at her, I feel my breath catch, the way it does whenever I study her carefully. She is beautiful. Not because she's my daughter. No, that's not it. If she were a complete stranger I met on a bus, I would think that she was absolutely the most perfect girl I'd ever seen. I'm serious. I remember when she was born, how lucky I'd felt at having a baby all the nurses went crazy about. As the years went by, she'd gotten even better looking, not like some children who become awkward, their features flawed by acne, or at best, ordinary looking. Now, at sixteen, she has perfect skin, perfect bone structure: she possesses the kind of haunting beauty that you know is not transient. She will be a ravishingly beautiful woman at my age, thirty-some years from now – unlike me, who started losing my looks in my late twenties, after smoking and drinking and general hard partying took their toll.

She darts a quick look at her boyfriend again and tries to suppress another secret smile. The boyfriend, cool and dark like a Maroon, his hair the texture of a Brillo pad, smiles encouragement at her before lowering his eyes to his plate. I look at his salmon-coloured shirt, which is loose about his skinny chest and exposed ribs. It is too loud, out of place among our sea of conservative whites and greys. I want to distrust him. I find, though, that I can't. There is an air of fragility about him that makes it hard for me to do so. They attend the same high school and have been dating for not quite a year, and although I'm glad

42

that they make an effort to keep their actions transparent by constantly being at the house, I still worry because I think they are having unprotected sex. Children today just don't realise the mishmash of consequences there are for irresponsible behaviour. For God's sake, they don't even think of oral sex as real sex. In my time we didn't even know the term oral sex. The only thing we knew to worry about was unwanted pregnancy. These days, there are so many scary things: AIDS, STDs, and what-all else. And although I credit my daughter with some common sense, I remember too well what it is to be sixteen and recklessly in love.

My stomach clenches, but I swallow that feeling of déjà vu and make myself think about other things.

Poor Gareth, meanwhile, is sharing out the food and steering the conversation – like a hotel's entertainment co-ordinator. He knows he has to assume the role of host on these occasions, keeping the topics light, neutral, because I am useless when my parents are around. Certain topics are off-limits. For example, my daughter is sensitive about her boyfriend, and what she refers to as the "bourgie" way we address him, which is just obscure teen-speak for the fact that she is ashamed of our very middle-class existence and the fact that we have worked our tails off to provide her with the kind of lifestyle she takes for granted.

Gareth valiantly pinch-hits on religion and politics (two glaringly non-light, non-neutral issues), at a loss to supply other mentally stimulating conversation pieces that can appeal to the broad cross-section of interests represented at the table. He may not be the world's best conversationalist, but I am grateful for his effort. He flounders, rallies, and then flounders again, like a drowning man. He makes some crack about Judaism, which is met with chilly silence. My mother nibbles delicately on her rubbery chicken, holding her fork like it's some strange, exotic piece of silverware she's unaccustomed to. She blithely ignores Gareth, as she always does.

My father, whose meds have obviously begun wearing off, tremblingly puts some rice and peas into his watery mouth and issues suspicious glares around the table. He was diagnosed a few years ago with Parkinson's. He has also recently suffered a stroke which has left him without the ability, or, I've begun to suspect, the desire to speak. Seeing him now, I am surprised at the rapid decline. I remember my father being something of a rake when I was growing up. He was a brilliant chartered accountant, up until the time of his retirement, shortly after which he and my mother migrated to Canada. For an accountant, he had a devilish combination of brains and sex appeal. There had always been women. His soulful, grey-green eyes drew them like moths to a flame. A scar on his face added an air of mystery. Square-jawed and broad-shouldered, he'd worn his dark, double-breasted suits with the regal bearing of a silver screen actor. I remember one occasion when my mother packed us children up in the middle of the night and left him. I was nine, Yvonne thirteen. We drove on and on into the night. From the backseat of the car, I watched light posts and banana fields hurtle by. My stomach trembled as we ascended winding country roads and crossed narrow bridges like fugitives in the night, until we ended up at my grandmother's home in the country, where we stayed until he appeared a few weeks later to take us back home. The night of our arrival I'd eavesdropped on my mother tearfully whispering to my grand-mother. The following morning when I followed my grand-mother out to collect eggs, I asked her what the word adultery meant. She glared at me and said, "It means your father can't keep it in his pants."

Now there's no trace of the old Casanova – just a very decrepit old man with a stooped, halting manner, whose eyes have taken on a hooded, clouded-over appearance so you are never quite sure if he is really there. I know that he is deeply resentful about having lost his alacrity. He is 72 years old, four years older than my mother, who, in her white, raw-silk pants suit, looks more like my older sister than my mother. I worry about them both. I worry about him becoming totally dependent on my mother.

I glance up at Gareth, my teddy bear of a husband, whom I have been in love with now for over twenty years. His hair, which has begun to lightly grey, is thinning on top. He's never been classically handsome. He is squat, like a pugilist, or maybe a bodybuilder gone soft, with rounded, meaty calves and biceps. These qualities don't seem so bad now, at his age. I notice he is sweating through his beige lightweight linen shirt; his top lip is beaded with moisture. The conversation has sunk before even slightly taking off. He turns over a few grains of rice with his fork and looks up and says, "Well, I mean, Jews and blacks in America should get along better. I mean, culturally, they have a shared history of suffering–" His voice trails off helplessly.

Oh my God, I think, and close my eyes. I can tell that he knows he sounds puerile. Gareth was never a scholar. He dropped out of school early to learn the mechanic trade, parlaying that knowledge into a successful business. He's still insecure in conversation around my parents, educated professionals who over the years have barely disguised their scorn for him. He blinks rapidly. An awkward silence descends over the room. He quickly shovels some food into his mouth and tosses me a look that is at once beseeching and pathetic. I look away. I cannot offer him succour. My glance flits outdoors to the nativity scene spread out on my neighbour's front lawn. My poor husband. I cannot help him.

My parents have never really forgiven me for marrying a downtown boy. It hits me. This is why Gareth and our daughter's boyfriend have forged an alliance. He is simpatico. When CeCe first brought home the boy, I had objected to his unkempt appearance, his less-than-stellar grammatical constructions. "What is that girl thinking?" I had asked angrily that night after we'd turned in. I was sitting at my dressing table brushing my hair, thinking about the new tension between CeCe and me. I could hear her muffled giggles in her room. She was speaking into the cellphone her father had recently bought her. More than likely to the boyfriend. Gareth, who'd just come out the shower, gently took the brush from me. Bending to whisper in my ear as he slowly brushed, he'd said, "Leave him alone, Mich." Then he'd distracted me the best way he knows. He lifted my hair and began running the tip of his tongue in concentric circles down the back of my neck until I began to moan. Now Gareth looks helplessly in the boy's direction, in need of a lifeline. He has no luck. The boy and CeCe are lost in their own arcane world of *Twitter*, *Facebook*, computer games and tech talk and what have you.

A wind whips up out of nowhere and startles us by slamming shut a window. At the same moment my twelve-year-old son, Jason, spills his glass of sorrel onto the white, lace-edged tablecloth. My last child, my sweet overweight baby boy who will someday soon, I hope, lose his baby fat. I can't help but to explode. "God, Jason, why are you so fucking clumsy!" I say between gritted teeth, and immediately wish I could swallow my tongue. The child looks at me with fear in his eyes, his lips trembling. I almost never swear within earshot of my kids and certainly never directly at them. My heart expands with regret for humiliating him but I stubbornly remain speechless. There will be enough time to apologise later, after my mother has gone. I watch him, the spitting image of his father, picking moodily at his food.

"Michelle!" my mother says. "For God's sake, what's wrong with you? Just take it easy!" She carefully places her knife and fork at the edges of her plate and looks over at me with frightening *sang-froid*. She goes to the kitchen and returns a moment later with a wet towel and rubs at the spot with palpable resentment, the jewels on her wrist flashing. I feel like a child again and the bane of her existence. When she's completed the task, she takes her seat in annoyed silence. I glance at Gareth, who averts his eyes, inspecting the food on his plate. He attacks a bit of the overcooked ham with gusto. Now it is he who cannot help me.

It is at this juncture that my daughter decides to deliver her news. She clears her throat in a theatrical manner, which sounds comical, since a deadly silence permeates every crevice of the room, the CD having mysteriously stopped. She clinks a fork against the side of her glass. "Attention, everyone," she says, and giggles. My heart nose-dives to my shoes. My daughter is famous for her bad timing.

"We have an announcement to make," she says, smiling, like a queen on her throne, bestowing a beatific smile on us, her lowly subjects. I swallow hard. "I'm going to have a *baby!*" she shrieks, unable to keep it in any more. She says it as though a baby is the latest pair of jeans or handbag she's procured from the mall.

She has no clue.

My baby is going to have a baby. She is only a child herself. What is she thinking about? CeCe can't raise a child; she's flighty, unfocused. Frankly, she shouldn't even be having sex. I suspected she was, but I assumed she was smart enough to know to protect herself. But something in the way she's grinning makes me think this pregnancy is no accident. What about her future plans? University? Beyond that? Does she not know that she doesn't need to be with a man and have his baby to be of worth in this world? Haven't I failed as a mother if I haven't taught her this?

Gareth's chair scrapes against the floor when he leaps out of his seat. "Baby," I say, putting out a restraining hand and rising halfway out of my chair. For a split second I imagine him going over and hitting the boy, knocking him from his chair and on to the floor. But he just ignores me, throws his napkin down on the table and walks out of the room.

There's a horrified silence.

"Excuse me," I say, standing up.

"Michelle," my mother starts.

My father looks even more confused.

"Mother," I warn, putting up an index finger.

I find Gareth in the tool shed behind the house. He's wrestling with the lawnmower, trying to prise it out from where it's stashed away in a corner. This is his way. He doesn't look up when I approach slowly, as if afraid of disturbing a skittish animal. "I want him out of my house," he snaps.

"Gar, we're not disturbing the neighbours on Christmas Day."

Gareth glares at me. "Take that boy home, Michelle."

"Sweetie, you're upset –"

"Oh, I'm upset?"

I stop for a moment, regrouping. "This isn't the worst thing that could happen. It's happened to other families…"

Gareth pushes the mower past me. I reach out for his arm. "Please, honey. You're not going to mow the lawn now, disturb the neighbours."

"I want her out of my house, too."

"What?" For a moment I think I haven't heard him correctly.

"I want that whore out of my house."

"What did you… did you just call my daughter a *whore*?"

"I know you know the meaning of the word." His voice is ugly, one I don't recognise.

Without thinking, I slap his face with all the force I can muster.

He doesn't miss a beat when he hits me back. Then: "Oh God, Michelle. I'm sorry –"

"Fuck you," I say.

Back inside the house, my mind is whirling, tears stinging my eyes. I run upstairs and into my bedroom. In the bathroom, I run the tap, hold a washrag under it and dab my eyes. Gareth has never before laid a finger on me. But for now, there are the people at the table downstairs. How can I face them?

I have to confess something I'm embarrassed to admit, but my first thought when CeCe spilled the beans was: "I'm too young to be a grandmother." I stare at myself in the mirror and say aloud: "I'm finished raising children."

I start, as though someone else has spoken these words. Then an image comes to me sharp and unbidden. I have not thought about this time in my life for many years.

The year is 1978. I am in my old bedroom, at my parents' house. I have just sat my GCE 'A' levels. I am eighteen and pregnant. My mother is standing at the foot of my bed. In the living room just outside my door, my father is sitting at the table, strewn with papers, helping a client with her taxes. He is oblivious to the conversation that's taking place only a few metres away.

I look at my mother's feet, at her fabulous stiletto heels. I block out the images that have taunted me since that day. The image of him and me in his kitchen, at the sink, him behind me, pressing slowly into me, my throbbing pubis against the lip of the counter. Him inching further and further into me, silken and open to receive him, giving it all up to him. Me, gasping when, at the end, semen trickled warm and sticky out of me.

My mother is telling me that the procedure will be done in Miami because the risk of someone here finding out is too great. I note there is no apparent concern for my safety, only that someone might find out.

The bedroom is as warm as a womb. She shows me the plane tickets. We will check into a hotel and while I have the procedure, she will try to get a spot of shopping done… "Might as well kill two birds with one stone," she says.

The procedure. She will not say the word. It will sully her lips to say the other word.

"Your father thinks we're going shopping overnight. He doesn't need to know anything else."

I nod because I can't think of anything to say.

And that is that.

On the plane ride back home I am cold and empty; my insides have been scooped out. My mother pats my hand and whispers reassuringly, "You'll thank me for not wasting your life, Michelle." My mother has great plans for my future. "You'll be glad you didn't waste it on that nothing boy."

A nothing boy who had no business loving me, a something girl.

A shudder runs through me now. I'd never admitted the truth to my mother: that Gareth wasn't the father of my unborn child. I'd never told Gareth about any of it, either, that I'd been screwing around on him all the time he thought we were being exclusive. I'd always been afraid to consider what Gareth would do if he knew. What I've continued to do with that other man, on and off, since we've been married. The fiction is that Gareth and I do not keep secrets from each other. Now, I wonder, based on his reaction in the shed, is there a secret he's keeping from me?

At the table I sit down, pick up my knife and fork and begin to eat food which is cold and has lost its flavour.

"Mom? Mommy?" CeCe's voice is tiny, her bravado dissipated.

Every eye in the room is turned toward me. I look at CeCe and see her staring at me with her big brown eyes, liquid, expectant. She has locked hands with the boyfriend, who, in a flash of clarity, I see I've labelled as a nothing, too.

"Mommy?"

Beside her, my mother flutters her napkin at her mouth and clears her throat. She is about to speak but I put up my hand to stop her. Secrets, I think. The private lives of girls and women. There is a hole opening up in my chest, but this is the chance I get to be a mother who loves unconditionally, who loves well. From where I sit, I can see a car cruise slowly by, its tyres sloshing against the asphalt. The rain has stopped again and there is a hint of sun appearing in dappled spots through the trees. This picture suddenly strikes me as perfect, and in order for the spell not to be broken, I close my eyes and hold my breath.

INDEPENDENCE

The summer of my thirteenth year, my father took me on a trip to the country for Independence weekend. He'd left us, finally, the year before, and I knew he was a busy man. He had a motor vehicle dealership – one of the biggest and, I might add, most successful in the entire island circa 1989 – and a girlfriend he was about to start another family with. But he cleared his schedule for me, for the big holiday weekend.

Quality time with you, Princess, he said, making my heart sing.

He'd had to sweat it, though, to get my mother's permission to take me away, on account of her finding out that on my last visit, he'd had his girlfriend staying there at the house with us. Adrienne was a narrow, brown-skinned woman who spoke with a funny accent that really was not so much an accent as it was some awkward mingling of broad St Elizabeth patois and a distorted Standard English. Pretty messed up, but, like my mother always says, don't judge. The truth is I didn't mind Adrienne. She was always cool with me. She was friendly, quick to smile, showing that little space between her front teeth, which drove my father crazy. He would tell her this, hoarsely asking her to stick her tongue through it, when he thought I wasn't listening. I could see how in love they were, even though they tried to act like they weren't whenever I was around. I'd been reading romance novels since I was ten, but now I knew what "smouldering looks" really meant. That Christmas I also had a good idea what they were doing when I heard them at night through the walls of the next room. Adrienne was everything my mother was not: sexy, young, pretty. She was small, almost my size, but with enormous breasts.

She wore glamorous outfits that I admired; she even allowed me to wear some of her clothes when we went out.

Naturally, my mother hated her.

It was me who'd stupidly let slip that Adrienne had stayed at my father's home that Christmas. I hadn't meant to tell my mother because I knew how psycho she could get. I felt bad, felt like I'd let my father down. I backpedalled, tried to undo the damage. I told my mother that Adrienne had only been there to help with the cooking and baby-sitting for me during the days when my father went to work. "Did you want him to leave me alone, unsupervised, in that big old house?" I asked, widening my eyes dramatically. It was true. Up in the hills where he lived, there wasn't a neighbour around for miles, and despite the thousands of dollars he'd spent on electronic security doodads, one could never be too careful. (It wasn't that he didn't trust me to be on my own, let's get that straight; after all, I was practically a teenager.)

What I didn't mention to my mother, though, was that Adrienne stayed shacked up in my father's bedroom at night, and that she'd confided in me, even before she did my father, that she was going to have a baby. All I said was that Adrienne was the one who had prepared all my meals, and not the helper – but my mother guessed. She was livid, calling Adrienne every name in the book. I'd never heard her use curse words before, and while I was sort of impressed, I was still annoyed with her. It wasn't Adrienne's fault that my father had left my mother.

"As long as your father insists on seeing that *whore*," she said, her lower lip trembling with rage. "You're staying right here with me. In this house."

The word hit me, almost physically. Whore. It was unfair. Adrienne never had a bad word to say about her. Believe me, there had been many times that she could have. My dad would sometimes complain about my mother, about something she did to annoy him. But Adrienne only made excuses for her.

Eight months later, my mother was still pissed off. But at least she'd agreed to let me visit with him again. It would be only be for a few days – the long Independence weekend – a belated birthday gift for me.

Baby steps, I told myself.

The conditions were strict: Adrienne would come nowhere near us, I was not to be fed fast food, and he would have me back home early Monday evening, Independence Day, four o'clock, in time for dinner, no excuses.

Daddy was prepared to do the silly little dance she always needed him to do, to lord it over him. "Yes, Marie," he kept repeating quietly as she laid down the law.

My mother, who was in the process of scrubbing the house from stem to stern when he came over, glared at him. She could have hired a maid to do the cleaning with the maintenance money she got, but, as my father pointed out, she had a persecution complex that she rode like a rented mule, and jumped on at every opportunity to make him feel guilty that he'd left her.

She had gotten fat since their break-up. Really fat. She had not once been out with another man in that time, and my father said she'd forgotten how to make herself look nice for a man. She wore a tatty floral housecoat, her hair tied with a greasy scarf. She stood staring Daddy down from the other side of the kitchen counter, and I couldn't help seeing her the way he did.

She shook out a nerve pill from the dispenser she kept next to the fridge and swallowed it without water. "I mean it, Jack. You don't have any more chances with me, if you muck this up."

My father looked over to where I was hiding behind the beaded kitchen curtain and winked at me on the sly. *Muck?* he mouthed, when she turned around. I shrugged, and gave him the thumbs-up sign, although secretly I felt that this negotiation made him come off like one of the losers who hung around outside his car dealership, begging for handouts. Still, it didn't matter. Neither of them had any idea how much of a treat it was for me to spend time with my father. The girls in my class at school got to see their fathers all the time. They complained about what nuisances they were, and how if the fathers weren't joining forces with their mothers to gang up on them, they just bickered with each other. But, as much of a pain as my mother could be, I would have given anything to hear both my parents bickering again – as long as they were bickering, together, under the same roof.

Friday dawned muggy and overcast. I was wearing a silly white summer dress with giant yellow sunflowers that my mother insisted I wear. The night before, we'd had a big falling-out over what my wardrobe should be. I wanted to pack only jeans. My mother, who hated that I was a tomboy, said I would be allowed only one pair. The rest were to be dresses and skirts. "You can stop rolling your eyes at me," she said. "You're thirteen now. Time to start acting like a young lady."

Seated in my father's new air-conditioned luxury Mercedes, which he drove like an old lady, I breathed in the new-car smell.

"Mummy hates this car," I said.

Daddy grunted.

"She says it's unfair you get to drive this and she's stuck with the Corolla. It broke down again last week, by the way. That mechanic is robbing her blind."

"Yes, well. I offered her a new car but she didn't want it."

I leaned my head against the plush leather headrest and thought about the T-shirts I'd sneaked in with my favourite jeans, and then about those dresses that were going to sit there in my travel bag, folded and untouched, until I came back into town on Monday.

"Find something on the radio, Princess," Daddy suddenly said. That was the best thing about my father. He didn't care about the music I listened to. My mother, who'd recently found religion, hated for me to listen to any "worldly" music. "Devil music," she said, mimicking the pastor of the Pentecostal church she dragged me to on a Sunday morning.

"I brought my own," I said, popping in a hip-hop mix I'd brought with me.

"Why the hell is there so much traffic? It's a holiday, for Christ's sake." My father was very big on "making good time", whether to school, work or a family outing. He'd been a soldier in another life. This was when he'd just come to Kingston. He had never gotten over his military training. He'd never been late for anything in his life. When we were still a family I remember him always impatiently checking his wristwatch, a big ugly round-faced contraption with a tan leather band, handed down to him from his father, which gave the times in four other countries, as well as barometric readings. I remember him arguing with my mother, who was tardy by nature. Which was why the ultimatum she'd given him about returning me home early was plain spiteful. I understood that she was just being a bitch.

We hit the Old Harbour bypass; in the distance the hills were brown and craggy and scorched by the prolonged drought. In the car, however, the air conditioning was set to high, the way my father always had to have it. Wet patches of condensation appeared on the glass.

"Christ," my father said, punching a button and adjusting his wing mirror. "We should have left earlier. The world and his wife will be heading to Ochi today. I told your mother to have you ready to leave by six. But no. *Six is too early*, she said. Jesus Christ. Just look at the traffic." He exhaled noisily, sucked his teeth.

I knew, though, that he wasn't mad at me.

I leaned against my door, so that I was facing him, pulling my legs up under me and draping myself with the oversize sweater my father had thoughtfully brought along, in case I got cold.

He was wearing mirrored aviator sunglasses and frowning at the road ahead, his square jaw set. He hadn't shaved but the stubble on his jaw gave him a dark and mysterious look. His thick, wavy hair was trimmed low. When he scratched his head with his thumb, I noted more grey hairs there now. His good jeans fit him snugly, and he wore the expensive white linen shirt that Adrienne bought him last Christmas open at the neck.

He was a good-looking man, it suddenly occurred to me. If I hadn't known it, I would have guessed his age wrong. He was not bad for an old guy. I looked again at his muscular thighs in his jeans and decided that he could actually be a star in a movie. Mrs WeeTom, the librarian at my school, who some kids had found having an affair with Mr Grant, our netball coach, would have gone for him in a heartbeat. I felt a secret pride. I even imagined my father's lips between my breasts.

As if reading my mind, my father glanced at me. He made a face but behind the mirrors I thought I saw him give me a half-wink. I looked away, suddenly uncomfortable. I don't know why, but it was a moment I knew I'd remember.

We drove on, listening to the music playing softly, and beneath it, the sound of tyres smoothly rolling over the road. I felt myself nodding off, drowsily snug beneath the woolly fabric of the sweater. I tried to fight sleep, not wanting to miss a single minute of the journey, but I was being pulled under, sucked into a black hole. There were so many things to catch up on. I wanted to hear about Adrienne, about his business and his employees whom I liked to see when I visited him at work. Then there were all the things I wanted to tell him about – school stuff. How much better I was doing in all my subjects, even French, which I loved but had never been able to get higher than a C. How I'd recovered from the sprain to my little finger and was able to play netball again. About Mrs WeeTom and Coach. Boys. I had a crush on Richmond Collins, a boy from my school I'd gone all the way with at a party but who wouldn't talk to me now. I was confused and wanted my father to tell me where I'd gone wrong, since I could not talk to my mother about sex or anything like that.

I awoke as we were passing a huge green neon road sign that read "Welcome to St Ann". The sweater blanket was still draped around me. I could tell that the temperature outside was blisteringly hot by the lines of vapour rising off the road.

"You're awake, sleepyhead," my father said, smiling grandly at me. He reached forward and turned on the air conditioner, which he must have turned off at some stage while I was sleeping, and ruffled my hair. "You slept right through the street parade, earlier." He crooked a thumb over his shoulder.

I spun around, peering hard down the street, as if I could summon up the scene. I'd been looking forward to seeing the dancing effigies of national heroes, grotesque and menacing because of their exaggerated sizes, the frightening *jonkanoo* I remembered scaring me as a child; I wanted to hear the drums my father said came down from our ancestors.

My father took his eyes off the road for a moment and looked at me. "This is fun, right, Princess? Just you and me, I mean."

I was filled with a warm feeling in my stomach. I remembered all the fun times we'd had together, as a family, before my mother had made him decide he had to move out. Despite the lengths she'd gone to –. her repeated reminders of the yelling and the arguments – to try to persuade me that I hated him as much as she did, I still imagined him coming back into our lives. I couldn't help myself. There were a million things I wanted out of life. To get picked for the national team was one. I wanted to grow bigger breasts, too, to be sexy like Adrienne. I wanted that badly. *Badly*. (I'd been secretly stuffing my brassiere since the second form.) But at that moment I could think of nothing I wanted more than my father coming back home. If I could have willed a genie to appear and grant me three wishes they would have been: "To get my father back, to get my father back, to get my father back."

My father had booked us in a resort guesthouse with a flower garden full of hibiscus, crotons, shame ole lady and bougainvillea in the front yard. That, unfortunately, was its biggest attraction. It was located on the outskirts of the town itself, with less than twenty rooms (it was smaller than the others in town). It had seen better times. Although the rooms were airy and the eastern ones had the distinction of being beachfront, the paint was peeling in places, the carpets threadbare and the linens faded. But it was the only place available for the holiday weekend at such short notice, and my father had only secured it because he was friendly with a booking agent who'd called him almost at the last minute, when a double reservation had fallen through. From the parking lot we could hear the sounds of children's laughter and water splashing in the pool at the side of the property. Tourists milled about, sipping fruity drinks with bendy straws, and there was an air of merrymaking. I grinned in relief at being with my father, glad to be rid of my mother. Away from her, I could begin to be myself, or anyone else I wanted to be.

The three days flew by, and it was Monday – Independence Day – time to go back home. The weekend had been great. Despite the crowds of lobster-coloured tourists and vacationers from Kingston crowding up the town, Daddy and I enjoyed ourselves. He was naturally easygoing, and wherever we went, he made me proud by making instant friends with the other vacationers who wanted to be included in the various activities we had planned for ourselves. Daddy was an outdoors man; we went horseriding, swimming and fishing with a group of tourists from the United States, Germany and England and a young couple from Kingston who had recently lost a baby. But he made sure that we got some time alone together, on Saturday, when we took a leisurely drive along the coast and watched the pink sun sinking in the sky on the horizon. I decided not to tell him about Richmond Collins; I didn't want anybody, not even some dumb boy who made love like a woodpecker, to come between us.

And then, on Sunday, our last full day together, we linked hands with our new friends and climbed the Dunn's River falls, picking our way up, almost to the top of the steep rocky incline of the swirling rushing water that stung our faces, slipping and sliding and squealing like schoolchildren.

On the day we had to leave, we both overslept. We'd stayed up late the night before, attending a pre-Independence day party the hotel had thrown. Daddy had begun knocking back Ochi Red Diamonds from earlier in the evening, which was probably why he did not stir when I went into his room, which adjoined mine, at seven the following morning. I'd gone back to my own room when he didn't budge and promptly fell asleep. When he finally knocked on my door half the day had already gone. I quickly tossed my clothes into my travel bag and went with him to lunch.

I was worried. It was already after one o'clock. I thought about my mother, at home in Kingston. She'd wanted me to spend some at least of the holidays with her. The deadline she'd given for my return wasn't entirely about being mean to my father. She genuinely wanted us to spend time together, maybe playing Monopoly or Snakes and Ladders. She'd said I was growing up fast, that I'd be graduating in a couple of years and before either of us knew it, I'd be leaving home. The problem was this, though. The out-of-towners would all be making their way back to the city later that day. We hadn't eaten yet. With the careful way my father drove the Mercedes, we would have to leave now, to get back to town before the four o'clock curfew.

Forty-five minutes later, we were sitting at a crowded dockside restaurant overlooking the sea. Sea gulls flapped up into the pale blue sky. On the white sand beach lovers strolled arm-in-arm. "Dad, maybe we can get doggie bags to go," I said, tapping the face of my watch, although I didn't want to leave.

Daddy laughed, recognising the familiar gesture.

"Relax, Princess. Stop cutting and swallowing your burger."

He had no concept of the jeopardy he was putting our relationship in. Either that or he didn't care. I couldn't bear to think it was the latter. Didn't he remember what happened last Christmas? Had it slipped his mind how spiteful my mother could be? How long she could hold a grudge? Hadn't he heard her shouting from the doorway in her housedress, huge pink setters in her hair as we'd pulled out the driveway on Friday morning: "I swear to God, Jack. If you don't bring her back on time this time, that's it!"?

My father made a face. "Princess Worrywort." Then, smiling through his hangover, he said, "I had a great time, baby." Through a mouthful of French fries, he added, "You did, too, right?"

"Yeah, Daddy," I said, trying to sound upbeat. "Fun. Lots. We should do it again, soon."

"Good," he said, sounding satisfied. He had dark circles beneath his eyes. He hadn't shaved; there was a shadow of stubble along his strong, square jaw. He reached across the table to pat my hand. "Eat up before they're too cold," he said, nodding at the fries on my plate. "And stop fiddling with your burger. You know this is your last chance to eat all this good junk" – and he winked – "before you get back home."

I couldn't answer.

"Stop worrying, Princess, I'll get you back in plenty of time."

Just then the cashier brought a portable phone over to the table. "There's a call for you, Jack," she said. He looked puzzled for a moment and with a giant swig of his Red Stripe, excused himself from the table to answer the call.

I watched him walking along the dock, in his pale pink Oxford shirt and snug-fitting jeans tucked into his scuffed tan workman's boots. He had an unhurried walk that involved a pronounced sort of pelvic movement and a kicking out of the feet that I'd begun to notice that weekend, when I saw the glances from women it attracted. I could see why women would think he was a catch. Now as I watched him I thought about the reasons that their marriage ended – outside women. She'd never said this to me, but it is what my mother had confided to her church sisters who came over to our house for prayer meetings. I never believed my mother then, but I could see now that she'd probably been right.

For a moment, I was almost embarrassed to look at him, as if I was doing something perverted. Like I'd stumbled across him naked, or thought about his lips on my breasts. I recalled how once he'd come to school to pick me up in a fiery red sports Trans Am, and how all the girls' mouths had fallen open as he whisked me away. The following day a rumour had begun circulating that I had a boyfriend who drove a Trans Am.

My father had lit a cigarette and was now waving his hand about as he spoke into the receiver. I felt an intense jealousy, remembering how he had spent the previous night flirting with a couple of white college-age girls we'd met earlier at the beach. The girls had laughed and danced with him, accepting the gin fizzes and strawberry daiquiris he'd kept plying them with. I watched him now and wondered who he was talking to. Probably Adrienne, though somehow I didn't think it was. Why would he have moved away to take the call?

I felt a burning urge to know him, to discover the secrets he was surely keeping. But you could never really know someone until they chose to reveal themselves, could you?

I didn't really know my father at all.

Just then he turned around and, shielding his eyes, searching to find where I was sitting, gallantly blew me a kiss. I could tell he was sweating. The St Ann heat was awful; it made it difficult to breathe, made you feel like a 200-lb man was sitting on your chest.

Holding my hands up over my head I pointed to my wrist again. He made a slight movement with his head, then continued to walk farther away. Minutes passed as he continued his conversation, smoothing his hair, stopping short, and then crushing out his cigarette beneath his heel, before hanging up.

"OK, Princess," he said, fishing out his wallet to settle the bill when he returned to the table. "Here's is the plan. I have to make a small stop before we head back. Don't worry. It's not far. Just in Galina. There's someone there I have to meet."

"But Dad-*dy*. We're late."

He ignored me. Instead, he grinned at the waitress, staring at her breasts popping out like two bald dwarves' heads over the top of her low-cut blouse. "Thanks, Jack," she said to him, sliding her tip beneath her bra strap. She smiled at him, sticking the tip of her tongue in the space between her front teeth. "See you next time you're in town."

I stood up, irritated. In the distance, a diver jumped from jagged rocks that jutted into the sea. "We have to leave now," I said bad-temperedly, and stalked off to my room to change my dress.

I remembered how after my father packed his things and left us, my mother's sister had come to stay for a few days. My mother spent the time stuffing her face with all kinds of junk: chocolate cake, ice cream, cookies. I'd overheard her say to Aunt Yvonne, weeping into a Kleenex, "You just don't know what it's like to be married to a good-looking man. The frustration, the way it makes you insecure and crazy."

My aunt had felt insulted and packed her bags and left. I'd thought my mother a bitch for saying that, but now I thought that maybe I understood what she meant.

As I looked at myself in the full-length mirror, I didn't know what annoyed me more: the fact that I was actually leaning toward my wretched mother's point of view about my father, or that I was seeing my father in a light I'd never seen him before. "Maybe it's this stupid dress," I said aloud, kicking the leg of the mirror, painfully stubbing my toe. It hurt for a long time after that, but somehow I felt like I'd struck a blow for my mother, for myself.

It was, by then, almost three o'clock. The drive back to Kingston would take almost two hours. We were already too late. Even if we could gun it and get there in an hour, there was still the stop we had to make in Galina.

Galina wasn't really that much out of our way; we would just have to take a different route back to Kingston, but one that would take a longer time because of the sorry condition of the country roads it followed.

The afternoon had begun to get cooler. The sun had all but disappeared as grey clouds moved in, though no rain fell.

My father was quiet for the first few minutes of the drive. Then he turned on the radio, started singing off-key along with the music. I giggled – his desired response. "My Princess Madeline," he said. He reached over and tickled my ear, something he liked to do when I was younger. He didn't know how much I hated it now.

"She's going to be mad, you know," I fretted.

"Your mother will understand," he said, sighing.

"Why do you love to provoke her?"

"Think I do that?" He sounded as though he was asking a question that he genuinely did not know the answer to.

"She won't let me go out with you again. We should've left earlier. But you had to take that stupid phone call and talk to that stupid waitress. And now we have to make this stupid stop."

My father turned the volume down and looked at me for what seemed an eternity. I was afraid he would collide with an approaching vehicle. "You're becoming your mother," he said. The four words he knew would hurt me more than any others.

I turned up the volume and looked out of my window at the scenery rushing by outside – the banana trees with their leaves swaying in the little wind that had picked up, the unaccompanied herds of sad-eyed cattle strolling along the side of the road, the occasional holiday motorist with a car full of joyriders. I squeezed in my anger until it formed a neat little ball in my belly.

My father tapped me lightly on my knee. "You were always so spunky, my little risk-taker. Don't let her get to you like that, Maddy. Don't let her make you a worrier, a stick-in-the-mud that no one wants to be around."

I kept staring out the window, pretending I hadn't heard him. He thought I was a worrier nobody would want to be around? He had no idea.

"Princess," my father said. "Look at me."

I turned around, looked at him, the way my mother would have.

"I know you don't understand a lot of the things that happened between your mother and me."

"I know it was about you and your women."

My father sighed and patted his breast pocket, feeling for his cigarettes. He stuck one in the side of his mouth and kept talking. He did this sometimes – stuck an unlit cigarette in the corner of his mouth – when he was feeling nervous or distracted. He'd never light up in his car. After a while, he pulled it out, waving it around before putting it back in the pack. "I know your mom will tell you all kinds of things about me, Mads, and I won't dispute a thing. Maybe you'll think I'm an awful person. And maybe you're right. But every man has his poison. Look, sometimes a man can love more than one woman at a time. When you grow up and understand a little more about life, you'll know that things aren't always black or white."

We had got to a particularly bad stretch of road. The car's wheels dipped and rocked jerkily over the potholes. We were both silent, enjoying the sensations the car was making.

"Why don't you call her?" I suggested. "All she ever wants, half the time, is just for you to call. Call her now and tell her we're caught up in a traffic jam. Make up something. She'll understand."

My father looked at me with something like admiration. "You know I can't. She'd ask too many questions."

Something in my expression made him go on. "But don't worry. I know how to soften up your mother. Stop worrying and just enjoy the ride, OK?"

I kept quiet, disgusted. He did know how to butter up my mother, wear her down, make her want him even when she knew she shouldn't. Something inside me flared, a quiet rage that felt as if it could burn me up from the inside out. How could he have spoken like that about other women to me, his daughter who loved him?

But that was many years ago, when I was just a girl. I'm a grown woman now with a life and a daughter of my own half a world away in Marseilles. I'm back in Jamaica for my father's funeral, and it's that Independence weekend I find myself remembering.

In the church my mother squeezes my hand, smiles encouragement at me when I look at her holding my child, her only grandchild, on her lap. She is still erect, her carriage regal. Her navy suit is tailored, a perfect fit on her now trim body. "It's OK, honey," she whispers. It has been a bumpy road but it led us to becoming the best friends we are today. I try to smile back at her through my tears. But she is a blur.

The chapel is crowded – standing room only. All around I can see my half-brothers and sisters, some I've met and others I'm surmising because of their resemblance to me. In the pew across from us sit Adrienne and her daughter Paula. My eyes meet hers while she's dabbing at her eyes with a frilly handkerchief, and she smiles, gives a little wave, before touching Paula and pointing to me and my mother. Paula, a self-assured teenager with my father's smile, salutes. They are like us, remnants of my father's past, relegated to second-row mourning behind my father's most recent family.

As the organ begins to play, I recall how eighteen years ago desire collided with duty. Some instinct had made me aware that the reason we were heading down that godforsaken stretch of back road with no streetlights was to meet some woman he had stashed away out here. By the time we reached the little clapboard house I was not surprised to see a barefoot girl, barely older than me, who could not keep her eyes off him. She was standing in the doorway, dressed in a shapeless frilly white peasant dress that hung off one thin shoulder. A little boy, also barefoot, whose features closely resembled my father's, clung shyly to the hem of her dress.

I was not surprised. Nor would I be, as the years passed, each time I met another of the many children he'd fathered with different women, both during and after the time he'd been married to my mother.

I remember closing my eyes as we coasted down those dark, bumpy, unfamiliar Galina streets, the already dwindling daylight slipping in and out of the leafy branches of ancient trees, solemn as judges, along the roadside. My father had begun singing again, in his good voice this time, his bass scooting around the music.

Later that evening, when we finally started out for Kingston, the burnt countryside blowing past us – the tall grasses by the side of the road swaying in the slight wind, a stream almost completely dried up by the drought, and, in the distance, a tiny white chapel on the edge of the bare, scabby hillside glowing reddish bronze in the warm evening light – I was sure of one thing: he was never coming back home.

I felt drowsy, the thrum of the car's engine oddly soothing. Sitting in the car earlier that evening as he'd flirted with the girl in the frilly white dress and cradled her little boy in his arms, I'd seen who my father was, and not who I wanted him to be. I felt sorry for my mother; I felt even worse for Adrienne.

My mother had been furious, of course, when we'd returned

well beyond the 4:00 curfew. But it was I who decided I didn't want to see him again.

Now all my anger has burned out. He was my father and, not unlike my mother, I loved him with a fierce helplessness I could not begin to explain. I knew that now. That weekend, I'd wanted to know the man my father really was; I'd wanted to know all his secrets. He was what he was: an unapologetic Jamaican loverman, a rogue bankrupt of honour and the ability to remain faithful to one woman. There was a hint of danger lurking in the depths of his dark eyes, but there was also compassion, tenderness, and charity, too. I'd wasted so much time hating my father. Now I understood what it meant to love such a man. But how could I possibly have foreseen the future and known then that I would end up in love with a man who was just like him, one who loved too many women, a married man with a family, a wife and daughters whose hearts he broke every day?

We drove on, that evening, the Mercedes greedily gobbling up the miles that separated us from my mother. "Happy Independence," he'd murmured, thinking I was asleep.

There, in the driver's seat, I knew he was grinning. This is the memory I want to have of him. If I close my eyes it seems I can still hear him say, "Relax, Princess, and just enjoy the ride."

COMFORT

The jealousy Sugar felt towards Celine was so acute it made her hair-roots ache. She was used to people, their own mother included, fawning over Celine. Without doubt Celine was the prettier, but she, Sugar, was the brighter. That should have counted for something, but in Plantation, mental acuity was not a priority. Early pregnancy, which Celine had just achieved, was practically revered. In the district, there were young girls, fifteen- and sixteen-year-olds, parading around the place, babies on their hips, already women. People spoke to them and of them with respect, these little itty-bitty girls who were heroic enough to take cocky. As if they were not the disgraced, unemployable secondary school dropouts and the eventual burdens on society Sugar knew they would become.

Sugar Crawford was twenty-two years old, older than Celine by three years, and still childless. A mule, she'd overheard people speculate, when they were unaware of her presence. She resented Celine for making them regard her with derision, and worse, pity, though she knew they would have thought her a mule, even without Celine getting pregnant. But it made her feel better to blame Celine. It wasn't that she wanted to get pregnant. She was ambitious and wanted more, much more, for herself. Still, it bothered her that, once again, Celine was the focus of people's attention, even if for the wrong reason.

The sisters scarcely spoke to each other now, and when their paths crossed at the once-weekly visits Sugar made to collect the eggs her mother sold to the hotel where she worked, she would ignore Celine, pretending not to notice the girl's growing stomach. Sugar also stopped bringing home the day-old, slightly bruised fruits and leftover food from the hotel kitchen because she knew how much her sister looked forward to this bounty. Sugar knew she had been described as loving and thoughtful, and at work she was regarded as a diligent worker who was always willing to go out of her way to help. So her present behaviour mystified her, frightened her even. How could she feel such an intense dislike – no, she should call it what it was – *hatred* – for her sister? Of her five sisters, Celine had always been her favourite, in spite of their mother's preference for her, the golden child. Sugar had learned to overlook all that. It wasn't Celine's fault that she was good-looking – her father was a handsome man. But now she couldn't stand the sight of Celine, who, with her little pumpkin belly, had become even more radiant in pregnancy, more serene, more beautiful – like one of those pictures of the Blessed Madonna Sugar had seen in books she'd read in Religious Studies. When she imagined Celine bouncing a tiny newborn infant on her knee, its skin all tender and sweet-smelling, her stomach tied in knots. She would then have to remind herself how a pregnancy would interfere with her plans. In Plantation, it was easy to forget dreams, which turned so easily into fairy dust when you were poor.

Plantation, located on the island's north coast, was a neglected agricultural town whose best days had long been behind it – that is until the building of the sixty-five-room Royal Twin Palms Resort, where Sugar had worked for the past five years. The hotel was modest by most standards – the rooms did not come fitted with phones and TVs and there were no group physical activities that were selling points at other places – but the atmosphere of intimacy and relaxation was what most visitors wanted. Sugar felt fortunate to be there. It was her first real job. The pay was not good; the hotel owners, an ex-pat family, who played hug-up with the government, were the ones who reaped all the benefits. But in part, at least, the foreign currency gratuities that the tourists gave made up for it. One Yankee dollar could fetch almost one hundred Jamaican dollars on the street, although the official exchange rate was a little over sixty dollars. Sugar's English was excellent, she had gone as far as grade nine in secondary school, with a keen aptitude for English language and literature. This made her popular with the tourists who did not have to waste time repeating things to her as they did to the other hotel staff, who they were often unable to understand. She earned a lot of tips working in housekeeping and sometimes at the bar. She ran errands and performed certain favours, from sewing loose buttons on their clothes, scouting ganja from the local Rasta hustlers she knew from the craft-market where her mother sometimes sold her Jamaica dolls to tourists, to babysitting for parents out for a romantic night on the town.

She also provided more intimate favours. White people on vacation, she discovered, were often uninhibited and intent on living out some tropical fantasy with willing natives. Sugar was no longer ashamed of the things she had to do; it was a living. Sometimes a couple engaged her to be with them. Other times she was paid handsomely by wives to service their husbands, or the other way around – by the husbands to watch her with their wives. Under inky night skies, in secret places both on and off hotel property, with the guests grunting above her, their pale sweaty skins slippery as frogs' bellies, she would think of all that the money could do. A baby did not fit into her plans.

Then, when Celine was about seven months' pregnant, apparently seized by a fit of depression, she carved a pattern on her cheek with a knife. She'd come back to the house, seemingly unaware of any pain, and their mother, looking in horror at the blood streaming out of the open wound on her daughter's face, had sent for Sugar. Adina Crawford was convinced that Celine's baby-father's other woman was working obeah on her. Too many strange things had befallen Celine – her skin had mysteriously broken out into boils, which would surface and then disappear, her ankles were swollen like an elephant's, and one day she'd woken up unable to speak because her tongue felt like a weight had been put onto it – what else could explain all this?

These things, Sugar tried to point out to her mother, might have been simply the consequences of the pregnancy: the boils, the swelling up, the depression. But Addie, in recent years a devoted churchwoman, was a strong believer in the devil, and she waved those reasons off. She had been pregnant nine times and had never once been sick; Crawford women were from sturdy stock. Despite her church's prohibitions, she engaged the services of a "woman" in the district, who instructed her what to do. She bought various oils and potions, which Celine refused to take, and when Celine objected to going with her to the obeah woman's parlour and taking a bath that would ward off the evil spirits, this was the final straw. Addie decided it was time for the girl to go to live with Sugar, whose earnings at the hotel had allowed her to move out of the cramped little two-bedroom house and rent a small flat not too far away.

"I can't do no more for that girl," Addie complained, and pointed to the battered suitcase she'd packed for her. Sugar looked at the graceless, knock-kneed woman her mother had become and tried to imagine her when she was younger. She found it hard to believe that her mother could have been pretty, and yet that was what Sugar's aunts and grandmother assured her. Men had loved her and earnestly sought her company. Was the evidence not there? Nine children with seven different men. Now Addie's body was aged and stooped, even though she was only forty, and her face was stern, with a mouth that seemed unable to curve upwards into a smile.

"What you looking at me like that fo', gyal?" Addie folded her arms over her emaciated, sagging breasts and stared pointedly at Sugar, her mouth set in an exasperated grimace.

Sugar stared unblinkingly back at her mother with a defiance that would have gotten her smacked in the face if she were younger. If Addie had been truly disappointed in Celine's lack of judgement Sugar would have been tempted to gloat, but she knew her mother was angry only because Celine's pregnancy was an inconvenience when she was already stretched to the limit trying to provide for her family. Addie, who depended in part on what Sugar gave her, but had no financial help from any of her children's fathers, mostly put food on the table by hustling: eggs to eating establishments and the hotel, coconut drops and gizzadas to the children's schools, and the like. But things were becoming increasingly tight.

Sugar looked down at the chamber pot that stood in one corner of the room – to catch the rain when the roof leaked. She had just got off work after a long shift and was in no mood to be bothered with this foolishness. Why couldn't Celine stay right there in her mother's house? She certainly didn't want to share her tiny flat with someone she hated. This wasn't how things were supposed to go; Celine wasn't her responsibility.

Addie turned abruptly and marched out of the front door and ducked into the outhouse. She'd started to lift her dress and pull down her panties before she'd even reached the door.

Sugar rolled her eyes. She wished she had a different kind of relationship with her mother. She appreciated how hard her mother's life was, even though she thought Addie had brought difficulties on herself because of the poor choices she'd made. She was often embarrassed by her mother's crude behaviour. She would still have pulled her pants down that way if strangers had been standing there in the room. Sugar had once been mortified to see her mother hike up her dress and pull aside her panties, exposing her thick pubic bush, before squatting down, legs wide apart, to relieve herself on the chimmy she kept beside her bed, in plain view of a pair of her church sisters who'd been visiting. When she was finished, Addie, instead of emptying the pan, had slid it under the bed.

At the hotel, Sugar saw mothers and daughters who described themselves as being each other's best friend. Mothers and daughters who laughed with each other, who shared secrets. Once, Sugar had been with a mother and her nineteen-year-old daughter whose bond was so close neither could bear the thought of being excluded from the other's island fantasy. As the mother held Sugar's legs apart over her head, making low moaning sounds as her daughter's silken blond head bobbed rhythmically between Sugar's legs, Sugar thought it was more than a little perverse but, secretly, also a little exciting. After that night she'd sometimes imagine being in bed with Addie and some suitor, Addie's minister, Elder Stevenson, perhaps. But these thoughts were fleeting. She would burn in hellfire for them, she knew.

She looked around now at the tattered sofa, the coffee table with the vase of dusty artificial flowers, the crowded whatnot stacked with the hideous figurines of animals, the picture of Jesus with the flame in his heart that hung over the doorway, the string festooned with old Christmas cards running from one corner of the ceiling to the next. She followed her mother out of the house.

Outside, a small wind blew the smell of chicken shit up her nostrils, making her eyes water. Wrinkling her nose, Sugar stopped in front of the outhouse door, which stood ajar. She kicked at the ground with the toe of her shoe, listening to the sound of her mother urinating.

"Mama, where I must put her?" she asked, knowing that her protests were useless. Nine children had lived in Addie's two-bedroom house; clearly, her one-room could accommodate both her and her sister. But she'd moved out precisely for the reason that she wanted space. She was very happy in her little flat; it was the first time she'd had any sort of privacy, the first time her actions weren't on display for her mother, brothers and sisters to comment on. But Sugar could not say this to Addie. Her mother simply wouldn't understand, or would write it off as Sugar being selfish and having highfaluting ideas about what life should be like. Sugar had always found it difficult to deny her mother's many demands because she hated her disapproval. She was practically the breadwinner for the large family – half of her fortnightly pay cheque went to Addie. Sugar did this without murmuring, but she resented this additional demand. "I don't have any space for Celine," she muttered beneath her breath. "She is big woman. She must go make her own life for her-own-self."

"Two spirit at war in dis house – the Lord and the devil," Addie said, briskly walking past her and back to the house. She continued in a loud voice for Celine to hear – she was sitting on the front porch staring dreamily into space. "I don't want no evil dwelling in here." She shivered as if she were tarrying for the Holy Ghost at the altar at church, squeezed her eyes shut and waved a hand heavenward. "Hallelujah! Yes, Lord. I wash my hands clean-clean from that in my house. You hear, Satan, I wash my hands."

Sugar looked out at Celine and made a *stchupsing* sound through her teeth – as much to register her annoyance with her mother's hypocrisy as her disgust for her sister. Sugar knew, although she had never admitted knowing, of those nights when Elder Stevenson had crept stealthily through the front door and crawled into Addie's bed. She stared at her sister's profile. Apart from the hideous bandage covering her left cheek, a reminder of the grotesque, self-inflicted wound, Celine's face seemed young and fresh, scrubbed clean like an innocent schoolgirl's. It was hard for Sugar to conceive that her younger sister had actually lain on a bed, beneath a man, and had been filled up with his seed. The thought sent a surge of something acrid rumbling through her, as if the thought itself had violated something sacred in nature.

Celine was still gazing at the darkening evening sky when Sugar, knowing it was pointless arguing with her mother, said, "Come, let's go."

The following morning Celine made breakfast for Sugar and set the table for her. "See, I mek a special breakfas'," Celine said, looking up, her face flushed from standing over the heat of the two-burner. The ugly yellow paint on the walls was peeling, the floorboards squeaking even more.

"No. I can't stop. I'm late for work," Sugar replied, trying to ignore the growling sounds her stomach was making. "You eat." She noted with relish that Celine looked disappointed.

Celine waddled behind Sugar, gingerly holding her back, taking her time to sit down on the old pea-green couch Sugar had gotten when the hotel had been refurbished. Sugar rolled her eyes, sighing. Celine was the laziest pregnant woman she had ever seen. Their mother had always been filled with boundless energy, even with her belly way out in front of her.

"Sugar," she moaned, glancing over at the plate and looking as if she were about to be sick. "I don't want to eat. I can't hold nuttn' down."

Sugar's patience snapped. "Don't eat, then," she said. "You can starve for all I care. Don't eat, and drop dead." She stalked out the front door, slamming it behind her.

In the following days, Celine lounged listlessly about the house in the same shapeless dress that needed washing, her hair uncombed, her beautiful copper eyes focused on the smoke coming from the glowing tips of the mosquito coils she had taken to lighting, like a ritual, throughout the course of the day. She refused to eat, fretting constantly about the baby's father, while being plagued by never-ending morning sickness.

Sugar's resentment for her sister grew; its chalky taste coated her tongue as she eyed her sister's growing belly and her thickening ankles. On sticky nights, when Celine stripped off all her clothes but her frayed panties, Sugar would stand over her little cot, watching her sister in tortured slumber, perspiration rolling down her skin, noting the prickly heat developing beneath the swell of her milk-engorged breasts.

One evening Sugar was about to go out with one of her tourists, a ruddy-faced athlete at a Florida university, who appeared at her flat with a bunch of flowers plucked from the hotel's garden, as though he was really a date and not paying her a hundred US dollars in crisp twenty-dollar notes.

The evening was clear and peaceful, with the smell of fragrant jasmine filling the air. Celine had dragged herself out of the house and was standing on the top step of the back stoop, standing on tiptoes, peering out towards the sea – which could be seen clearly from Sugar's backyard – when the tourist, picking his way around the side of the house, had startled her, making her almost lose her balance. Sugar, who had come up behind her that very moment, saw Celine wobble unsteadily before regaining her footing.

Later, moving silently beneath her date, on a craggy patch of pebbled earth behind the old courthouse across the road from the pier where they'd gone to watch cruise ships dock, Sugar ignored the man moving urgently inside her, making grunting noises, his white skin a startling contrast to her rich, dark one, and wondered whether Celine might have miscarried if she had fallen.

Sugar closed her eyes as the man eased out of her and, without pausing, flipped her over and hiked her skirt up further around her waist, grabbing a fistful of her hair before plunging roughly into her.

Sugar winced as the pain shimmied through her like volts of electricity, then willed herself to remain perfectly numb. Some of the tourists liked doing it this way; she didn't like it but backdoor would get her more money. It would soon be over, she reminded herself. To avoid concentrating on the pain, she imagined Celine lying in a heap on the ground, with amniotic fluid oozing into the earth between her legs.

Every fortnight, after she got paid, Sugar thought about what she needed the money to do. How would the little stretch? There was always something: fix a patch on her mother's leaky roof, help buy clothes for the children. Put aside money for going to Kingston to find Isaiah. In time, that became putting aside money for an obeah man who could help her bring harm to Isaiah.

Isaiah was the only man she'd ever loved. If he could be called a man. What kind of man declared his love for a woman and then went off to town and forgot about her? The letters had become vague almost as soon as he'd settled in at the rooming house he'd found with the cousin he'd gone to Kingston with. Big City life. Sugar knew she'd become too local for Ziah. She couldn't compare to city girls, who were sophisticated, educated, beautiful, who could hold the attention of any man. She could make a good home for a man; she was a hard worker, kept her house clean, clothes washed and ironed, plus she was an excellent cook. On her back, she displayed similar capabilities. She knew how to please a man. She'd been told she was gifted in that area. But maybe a man needed more.

Maybe Ziah needed more.

She remembered how they'd met, the first time they made love. They'd met a few months before, on the hotel property. Isaiah was the newest member of a team from the maintenance company responsible for the upkeep of the place. He was one of the men who mowed the lawns, and she'd seen him as she pushed her cart from the supplies department to the rooms on the eastern side of the resort. He'd been on a riding mower and, through the corner of her eye, Sugar, neatly prim in her powder-blue uniform, noticed him staring at her when he'd collided into a bed of roses. She had adjusted the volume of the second-hand Walkman she'd received from her date the night before, smoothed her skirt over her hips, and suppressed a smile. Later, she had made discreet queries in the kitchen about when the service would be back and made sure she was on duty that day.

Isaiah, it was soon obvious, was interested in her but he seemed unsure about how to advance the relationship. He would pluck a flower and shyly hand it to her before quickly returning to his crew to continue working. Or he would bring her a pack of banana chips – her favourite food, she said. He was about her age, skin the colour of drained engine oil, tall and lanky, all gangly limbs with ears like the handles of a jug. He stuttered, especially

73

when he was nervous, though that decreased the more comfortable he became around her. Sugar liked him immensely. She didn't care that he hadn't finished primary school, or that she couldn't speak to him about her favourite books, the way she could with her tourist dates, or even that he could not buy her the expensive gifts she got from them. When she lay in her little cot at night, her body still throbbing from a date's earlier mishandling, she thought about how much she wanted Isaiah and how nice it would be with a man she wanted to be with because she liked him and not because she needed something from him.

Their first time together had been in an unoccupied room near the back of the property that was used only when the hotel was full. It was smaller than most of the other rooms and not as attractive, but it had an unobstructed view of the night sea. Sugar reached early, aired it out, changed the bedding and filled an old orange-juice box with water and some butter-coloured hibiscus from the garden, placing it on the coffee table. Then she sat in a chair by the window and waited. Isaiah, who lived in a nearby district, had bummed a ride with a van man he knew, who was going on a night run to Kingston, then walked the rest of the way. He knocked quietly on the door. He was nervous, Sugar realised, standing there in the doorway, sweating and with no gift, but she put him at ease when she pulled him inside, and gave him wine she'd stolen out of the suitcase of one of her dates. She adjusted the thermostat on the air-conditioner, and soon they were on the bed, embracing, kissing. Sugar had spent a lot of time earlier that evening bathing and oiling her skin. She had lightly dusted her pubic hair with talcum powder and had spritzed perfume behind her ears and knees.

Soon, their clothes were off, scattered across the floor. Isaiah rolled on top of her and, straddling her, sinews rippling, gazed into her scrubbed face. "Sh..Shh..Sugar?" Isaiah had moaned when he eased inside her, gently, as if he was afraid she was glass and would break easily.

She wrapped her legs around him, pulling him deeper, further, into her. "Yes, Ziah?"

"I l..l..love you."

There in the darkened room, tears had leaked out the corners of her eyes and into her ears. It was the first time in a long time that she hadn't had to put on a show for a man, grunting perverse things she didn't really feel. It was the first time it felt real.

After the day Celine almost fell, Sugar could scarcely bear being around her. She could not look Celine in the eye. She was ashamed of the blackness of her heart, but she could not help herself – her jealousy seemed to be feeding like a cancer. Isaiah was not going to come back; there would be no family and a life together. She would get old and die alone. She began staying late at work, requesting double shifts and overtime, anything that would keep her from crossing paths with her sister. She was exhausted from the long hours spent working. Dark circles appeared beneath her eyes. She prayed her sister would hurry up and have the baby so she could go back to Addie's house and leave her and her unblessed womb in peace.

Then, one day at work, Sugar overheard two of the kitchen maids at the hotel gossiping about her. They were two older women she despised.

One of them said: "You don't hear how Sugar sister man making idiot outta her? The gyal big-big pregnant fi a wutliss, no-good man. Him have a woman that work at Mr Chin shop, see!"

The other one snorted. "That's what they get. Miss Addie gyal-pickney dem love to open they leg to too much man, you hear. You never know Sugar is the biggest whore? Oh, you don't know, chile? Is open secret the things she do fo' the white tourist dem. Her man leave her. Gone a Kingston. Don't want her no more. He must be hear 'bout her whoring ways. Yes, chile. Him leave before she could bring disgrace pon him."

The first one, chuckling louder: "Celine is the one that fool-fool, though. She let sheself get ketch. And don't have nothing to show fo' it 'cept big belly."

"Me hear her man won't have nothing to do wid she nor di baby."

"Well, that's 'cause him other woman, the dry-foot gal, Pauline, she have big-big belly, too. Patsy tell me sey she and her friends dem come 'a market the other day and she a talk how she obeah Celine."

Sugar felt something like a punch in her gut. From where she stood in the dining hall, she could see out the windows and across the sea. Sugar felt the red in her eyes, rubbed at them. She didn't care about what they'd said about her; after all, it was true. But the things they were saying about Celine hurt. She had never believed the obeah story before. But, instinctively, Sugar knew what she was overhearing was the truth. Celine did not deserve to be treated like this by the breadfruit head liar she'd made the mistake of getting belly for, who'd humiliated her by choosing another girl over her. Nor did her little sister, who was so good and kind and trusting, deserve to be discussed by a bunch of meddling gossips in that way.

Sugar turned and ran out the front door. At the front gate she stopped, rushed back toward the building and burst into the kitchen. The two women were still there. With a scream she ran toward them. She pummelled both of them with her fists, ripping at their hair, scratching at their eyes.

That evening Sugar sat with Celine on the back steps of the house in the thickening dusk as fireflies flickered and the stars appeared like tiny alien gods. She was still dressed in the grey hotel uniform.

"Come. You need to eat for your baby," Sugar said gently, trying to tempt her with a morsel from her plate.

But Celine only turned her head away and stared vacantly out into the yard at the mango trees, ripe with the smell of the fruit rotting on the ground beneath. In the distance, boats could just be seen, bobbing dots on the sea.

It was already late summer; most of the tourists were leaving to return to their homes and their normal lives. Sugar thought about snapping freshly laundered sheets and changing towels at the hotel. What was she going to do, now that she'd walked off the only job she'd ever had?

Two months had gone by since Celine had moved in. She was due any day now. She sat on the top step, above Sugar, who was seated on the bottom step, her face swollen and bruised. Celine looked at Sugar with interest. "Your face," she murmured, and stretched out a leg crisscrossed with tiny spider veins. Tentatively, she reached down to take a piece of yam from Sugar's plate and slowly began to chew it. Sugar brushed away her concern. "Don't worry about it," she said. "Just eat."

Sugar smiled at her sister, pretending not to notice the foul smell that came from her. "Both of us have frig-up faces now."

"I didn't do it, y'know, Sugar."

"Didn't do what?" She was a pretty girl, Sugar observed, as if seeing her sister for the first time. Even in spite of the scar, the pattern of a sickle, on her face. She had a straight nose with nostrils so tiny they must surely have made breathing difficult, and small pink lips that Sugar imagined tasted sweet on the lips of the fool she had given her innocence to.

"I didn't do it," Celine repeated, more urgently. She looked hard at her sister. "This –" She pointed to the ugly mark tattooed into the smooth skin of her cheek. "Him do it."

"What? Byron cut you?"

Sugar was surprised at the anger she heard in her own voice. She stopped speaking, not wanting her anger to escape and cause Celine to retreat. She leaned over and spooned some saltfish into her sister's mouth. Celine opened her mouth like a hungry baby.

Sugar's anger surged again. "I should go to his house and stab him," she said, and spooned some more saltfish into her sister's mouth.

Celine tried to lick at the spot where a dribble of oil had splashed onto her chin with her tongue. Sugar wiped it away for her with her fingers, and Celine smiled gratefully.

For a while neither of them spoke. They both sat watching the late evening sky turn from pink to indigo. Sugar had always heard the tourists say the Jamaican sky was magical, that it was the most beautiful sky in the entire Caribbean. They said that there was a place in Negril where you could see straight to the edge of the world, where hundreds of tourists converged each day to watch the sun setting, and divers plunged recklessly from the cliffs to the depths of the sea beneath, besotted by the *goozoom* of the Jamaican sky. That evening Sugar almost believed it was true.

Celine was still staring into the distance, thoughtfully chewing the food in her mouth, like a cow her cud. When she swallowed she looked back at Sugar. "He never mean to," she said, her eyes clouding over. "I was mad. I go to him with a knife. We start to fight." She clutched Sugar's hand and looked pleadingly at her. "Him was defending himself against me. He grab my wrist, trying to get the knife. In the scuffle, it accidentally end up hitting my cheek. He never mean to. That was the last time I see him." She buried her face in her hands and started to cry.

It was Sugar who noticed the blood running down Celine's legs. She gently shook the girl. "Come," she said, trying not to panic her. "We have to find Mama."

Back at home, Sugar bathed Celine. There was no water in the pipes so they had to make do with the enamel pan that was filled with water from the cistern outside. She noted with bemusement that Celine's belly was still remarkably far out in front of her although there was no longer a baby in it. The last time she had bathed her sister, Celine was a little girl with a tinkling laugh and coloured ribbons at the ends of her plaits, wriggling as Sugar tried to soap her up. She had always been burdened with the responsibility of taking care of the younger children, while their mother sold her crochet pieces and stuffed calico-cloth Jamaica dolls at the craft market in the town square. Now Celine sat meekly as Sugar's fingers moved tenderly over her body.

Tears began streaming down Celine's face. With a start Sugar realised that she, herself, had been crying, that Celine had probably taken her cue from her. What kind of older sister was she, anyway? She remembered the time she'd fantasised about Celine losing the baby. She got in the pan, fully dressed, beside her sister and loosened her plaits, washing the stink out of her hair with the scented soap that she'd been given by one of her tourist dates. He was a huge Boston college professor with skin as red as a boiled lobster's who complimented her on how "pretty" her English was and had given her flowers as though he were a suitor.

Shadows fell against the wall. Outside, they could hear the rumble of a delivery truck from St. Ann's Bay on its way to the hotel. Sugar splashed the last of the water onto Celine's head and the girl closed her eyes tightly and shivered.

"OK, Celine," Sugar said, putting an arm around her sister, but Celine did not move.

The night had become cold and they sat, shivering, clinging to each other for a long time, until there were no tears left and there was nothing left to do but get up.

FALLING BODIES

A hotel bed in Miami on a Saturday night is probably the worst place to be if you're by yourself. Which is why I was painting my nails Luscious Lavender in a lumpy, crumb-filled bed, way up on the 24th floor of The Miami Colonial, the air conditioner blasting so cold it was making the polish thicken right there on the brush. I said a curse word out loud – something I try not to do; the sound bounced hollowly off the wall, depressing me even further.

I was in Florida with a group from my office, for a trade expo and convention. There's nothing as invigorating as hot, dry air on your skin, the feel of cold ice cream on your tongue, the smell of sea salt in the air – and Miami's just place to experience it. But here I was, alone with an empty box of chocolate chip cookies. The rest of the group had gone out clubbing with my boss, an Englishman who was, according to him, a "Miami nightlife *aficionado*". Yes, he used that exact word. But then, with a badly pock-scarred face, he would. It was our last night in Miami, so this was their one shot to blow off some steam after the hectic few days. Mr Cromwell had rented an SUV and they'd all taken off, determined to milk the night for all it was worth. They would not be back until the wee hours. I stayed back because I hated them. It was bad enough to be stuck in the same room as Althea and Samantha, account executives who made my life at work a living hell. I wasn't going to doll up to go catting it up with them and Mr Cromwell and Dennis and Pruitt, all of whom, after a few drinks, would start getting grabby. They were always just a hop, skip and jump away from a sexual harassment lawsuit, judging from the rumours that flew around the cafeteria and ladies' bathroom at work. There were three guys to three of us girls. I did the math. I guess they'd made the calculations, too. I wasn't interested. A workplace fling is always a bad idea, even if it's done a thousand miles away. I have previous. Whatever, nobody was going to get lucky with me.

I stayed behind, really, because I wanted to be alone. Personal stuff – about me and Eric. Sometimes you have to go away to see things more clearly. But then again, revelation is sometimes too much. Like looking directly at an eclipse.

Eric and I had known each other for eight years; we'd been together for almost five, married for three. Our marriage was in what was referred to as being "in crisis", because of my affair. This was with an old boyfriend. He'd come in to Kingston for six months, on some kind of job training, and when it was over, so was our affair. He returned to Montego Bay, where he lived with his wife and three kids. He was moving forward with his life. I told Eric I wanted to move forward with mine. It was stupid of me – the affair. But that's me. I do stupid, risky things all the time. I don't know why. Eric was the best thing to ever happen to me, and I had to find a way of messing it up.

Eric wanted to know why I'd done it. I told him I'd been lonely, bored. I know it sounds like an excuse, but it was true. Eric had been promoted to police inspector and worked extremely long hours. It's hard being married to a man who was at work when I was home, and home when I went out to work. I could not get used to it. I spent birthdays, anniversaries, Christmases alone. This may sound trite, but it is the truth. I was lonely. So, when my ex-boyfriend called me up, out of the blue, things just sort of naturally progressed from there. I hadn't spoken to him since we graduated from university. At school, he'd been one of those come-around guys I let have sex with me, even knowing he'd go back and tell his friends. He was from money, handsome and popular. But he'd never taken me out; we'd always stayed in his room in hall. When he called me up, I'd forgotten about the humiliation he'd caused me when we were little more than children. He caught me at a bad time; it was the end of the year, the time I was most prone to being depressed. I visited him in his hotel room after work one evening and watched him lose more and more of his clothes as the evening wore on, and everything went to hell from there. We even had sex on the pool table in the games lounge. Then we took it back to his room, where he kept having to cover my mouth and say "shhh," when I came, screaming his name out loud. I was so ashamed I couldn't bring myself to go home, and ended up staying with him until three in the morning. Later, after the affair ended, when I told Eric this, tears shimmered in his eyes. I don't know why I told him this detail. It was sadistic and cruel. Eric deserved someone better.

"It's over, though, baby," I said. "I swear to God."

He didn't answer.

In the distance we could hear neighbourhood children playing, shrieking in the street. When he finally spoke, he said, "And I'm supposed to be the detective." He laughed bitterly through his tears, snot running into his mouth. He was sitting on the edge of our bed, still dressed in his work clothes, his balding head bowed. His revolver was between his legs, the way he carried it while he drove his car.

In the beginning, I'd been charmed by his ability to be vulnerable, non-macho – unlike his police friends. Now, his crying nauseated me. On my knees before him, I remembered those glorious months with my ex – all the sex, the variety of positions we'd been too unsophisticated to try while we were in school, positions that even now I would never consider with Eric – and felt ashamed all over again. "Say something," I begged. "Yell at me." I tried to guide his hand to pick the gun up, aim it at me.

But of course he didn't; he never would; he was a good man, a decent man, and he truly loved me. He looked up and blinked rapidly instead, then turned his head and stared out the window so I would not see his tears.

A few weeks later, I missed my period and bought home pregnancy tests before going to my doctor, who confirmed that I was pregnant. It wasn't Eric's and I was positive he'd never stay if he knew this. I did consider passing the baby off as his but he and the baby's father had such different physical traits. I didn't want to complicate things even further, but I just didn't know what to do. This was the stuff I was stewing over on the 24th floor.

I decided I ought to call home. I'd been trying to get through to him since reaching Miami and kept missing him. In spite of everything, I missed hearing his voice. Maybe we could put everything behind us with an ocean separating us. Maybe even talk dirty to each other on the phone, the way we did when we'd just started going out.

It was almost 9:00 pm, 8:00 Jamaica time. A half-hour passed and I was getting nowhere because the international circuits were constantly busy. I tried to imagine what Eric was doing but couldn't. What would we have been doing on a Saturday night in Kingston if he wasn't at work? Parked on a beach chatting and looking out at the calm waters? Out to a movie? Eating out at a fish fry or something? Mad with each other? Making love? No, definitely not that. It had been months since we'd had any sexual contact, which was going to be problematic if I decided to keep the baby.

I dialled again and slammed the phone down when the recorded voice of the international operator once again advised me that all the circuits were busy. I tried to summon an image of Eric in my mind, and found that I couldn't. What the hell! It had only been what... four days that I'd been away and already my life in Kingston seemed faraway, indistinct.

Frustrated, I eased aside the heavy brown drapes to look out at the downtown Miami lights. I thought about the little Cuban deli shop across the road from the hotel where I had stopped by each morning for coffee and triple-decker ham-and-cheese sandwiches. It smelled of cigars and played endless salsa music as customers shouted over the noise. Screw it, I decided, life's too short, and went to the bathroom and ran a bath, sitting on the toilet and examining the little veins on my legs while I waited for the tub to fill up.

Half-an-hour later, I tucked the room key into my bra strap, and wobbling in a pair of black stilettos which I'd packed for the trip, headed down to the hotel lobby.

I met Eric when I was held up and robbed at gunpoint on a bus, during my final year at university. He was the policeman who investigated the case. He'd been collecting statements from some other passengers who'd been on the bus when our eyes met across the room at the police station. And like that – *bam!* – he said he fell in love with me. I'd looked so vulnerable, like the bruised petals of a hibiscus, he told me years later. All he'd wanted to do was get the guys who'd made me so scared. I never got back my bag but I got him. He was older, which I liked. He was kind of geeky but I felt I had to stop making looks matter. I was sick of the come-around boys my age who only wanted one thing. Eric was relentless in his pursuit of me. He was interested but kind, respectful to me in a way no other guy had been. The fact that I'd been raised in a girls' home in a rough section of Kingston until I was taken in by a missionary couple meant nothing to him. Nor did the fact that the most I knew about my parents was that my mother was a junkie hippie who had visited the island from Sweden in the free-loving seventies but had never made it back home, and my father was the "native" artist/loser she fell in love with and who'd pimp her out when they needed money for drugs. "It's not where you come from," Eric told me, "it's where you see yourself going."

I was lucky to have him. I told myself this constantly, even when I was behaving disgracefully with my ex-boyfriend, or thinking thoughts of pure hatred towards his wife as the time drew closer for him to return to his life in MoBay. Eric had taken me when no one else would. And this was how I'd repaid him. I wasn't lonely. I was an ungrateful bitch who didn't love her husband any more.

The hotel lobby was buzzing with people. It was huge, beautifully furnished, with massive potted ferns in the corners. The marble floors shone. The chrome handles on the dollies the bellboys used to transport suitcases gleamed. I glimpsed my distorted reflection in one that rolled past, and wished I really was that skinny. I tried to ignore a sudden twinge of nausea – guessed I was fast coming up on the morning sickness stage, and it suddenly dawned on me that I really *was* pregnant, that if I went through with it, I would become someone's mother.

At the front desk, the receptionist was a beautiful Hispanic boy, thick eyebrows carefully plucked at the brow bone, slick sideburns, and impeccable manners. He was slight, his voice high-pitched. I could imagine him on his days-off, lounging around his apartment wearing flamboyant clothes with puffy sleeves, like Liberace, sipping vodka stingers.

I cleared my throat.

"Ah," he said, looking up, eyebrows arched, smiling, his straight teeth gleaming and white under the light. "Buenas noches, señorita." In Miami, people tended to mistake me for a Latina because of my colouring.

"Hi," I said, leaning against the counter. "What's there to do in Miami on a Saturday night?"

He looked at me in surprise, then told me with only the slightest trace of an accent the things I could do. "We provide transportation," he informed me, gesturing with a delicate, fine-boned hand. He winked, as if he was a Hollywood leading man. Little lines appeared around his eyes. "A *preety* girl shouldn't be alone, no, on Saturday night in Miami."

I looked at him, a gay man trying hard to seem straight. I smiled, tried to look eager, a party animal, as though I didn't have a baby inside me. Who was pretending to be something they were not?

I looked around. A pregnant woman was sitting in a corner, near a candy-vending machine, reading a newspaper. I wondered what I would look like with a pumpkin belly. My mind flashed on a schoolmate, Corrine Nevers, whom I'd accompanied to have an abortion, when we were in fourth form. I'd told myself I would never have one. Now, I wasn't so sure.

Everything the receptionist suggested had sounded good. There was Havana Nights, at some popular nightclub in little Havana, a Cirque du Soleil type of show that apparently involved dancing, a suds-making machine and a couple of good-natured drag queens, or there was Saturdays on the Bay in Lauderdale.

Outside, a taxi had pulled up and a man and a woman stumbled out. The doorman yanked open the heavy glass front door and they sauntered laughingly up to the front desk, arms linked, and asked for their messages. Up close, I saw that he was older, with greying hair – not one strand out of place – dressed in an expensive, double-breasted, pinstriped suit. He looked a bit like Christopher Walken. She was much younger – slim with olive skin and thick straight black hair that hung in a sleek ponytail down her back. Her dress was of a brightly printed material that looked like chiffon, flirty, cut low in the back as well as in the front. High heels showed off perfect calves. She kept giggling and nuzzling up to him while his hand roamed inside the low back of her dress. When she looked at him and smiled, he smiled back. He was married, I could tell, and she was not his wife. They were more intimate than Eric and I had ever been. Eric was older than me; not as old as the man, but still obviously older. I stood there watching then, even after they'd stepped into an elevator and disappeared.

I was thinking of going back up to my room – feeling ridiculous in the heels and the stupid cocktail dress that I'd bought earlier that day at a downtown dress shop – when a laughing, chattering group of people burst out through the doors of the hotel's disco, letting the pulsing beats spill into the lobby.

I turned around, and Jorge – as his brass name-badge read – smiled at me again. The room key cut into my skin beneath the bra strap. "They're waiting for you," Jorge said, making a sweeping gesture with his hands, as if he were a host on a game show, alerting me to some prize that I'd won.

The ballroom throbbed with the trippy, white sound of eighties and nineties music that I still adored, even now: Wham!, Tears for Fears, the Thompson Twins. Cigarette smoke hung in the air, curling about like mist. Lights from the giant disco ball over the dance floor made everything sparkly, alive, as if an adventure was lurking somewhere.

I sat at the bar and ordered a Sex on the Beach. It was the first time I'd ever ordered one. Miami was as good a place as any to become a different person. I watched a young black couple slow-dancing near the bar. The flashing lights fell by turns on their white clothes and their dark skins; I thought they looked beautiful.

For the next hour or so, I had guys sidle up to me, offering to buy me drinks. None of them interested me, certainly not enough to accept a cigarette and in return give a fake name and even faker laughter. The last one to approach me came up just as the bartender had lined up the fifth drink in front of me. He was a blocky man with sunburnt skin, a huge, bulbous nose, a weak chin and a smarmy smile. He insisted on buying me another drink, even when I politely turned him down. I made my jaw slack, let my tongue loll and some drool slide down the side of my mouth when I turned a cross-eyed stare at him.

The bartender laughed and high-fived me as the guy hurried away and I wiped the drool off my face with the cocktail napkin. He shouted, "You're fierce, girl! I like your style!" and went off to serve someone else.

I was alone, but now I didn't care. When I'd confessed to him, Eric had told me that I was so cold I'd end up that way anyway: alone. Besides, I didn't *feel* alone. There were a hundred other lonely people around me, sweaty, gyrating bodies trying to dance away the hole in their lives. Just being in the room with all that heaving mass was making me feel better. It was funny that I had to come all the way to Miami for that.

I turned back and tried to catch the eye of the bartender, who was at the other end of the bar. There were about five guys working the long bar, all young enough to be students. My bartender was a lanky guy with bad skin and tattoos on his arms. He wore a vest and a dog collar around his neck. He smiled and waved when I raised my glass to him.

I was on to my third drink and drinking too fast, because the ice had begun to melt in them and they were turning watery. Then it occurred to me I shouldn't be drinking at all in my present condition. I'd read about foetal alcohol poisoning. My head felt light, too, and I remembered I hadn't eaten all day, but was too far-gone to care.

I thought again about Corrine and our visit to the doctor's office. She'd been loopy from whatever they'd given her but it had all been over in a matter of minutes. We'd never spoken about it again, but it was something I'd thought about from time to time. I remember the wild look in her eyes when she'd confronted me that day in the bathroom and told me she'd missed her period. We hadn't been that close – I was not particularly close to any of the children at high school because I was afraid they'd find out where I lived and tease me about it. Corrine was a tall, good-looking girl who sat beside me in Biology. She ate the expensive cooked lunch with the other rich children in the cafeteria while I ate a sandwich or crackers under the trees, and she'd stared through me when she drove past in her father's shiny black BMW as I stood at the bus stop. The longest we'd ever spoken to each other was when she asked to borrow my notes when she'd missed class; once she'd asked if she could copy the words to a Peaches and Herb song that I'd written on the front of my folder.

I was so caught up with thinking that I didn't notice that someone had slid onto the stool next to me and was munching nuts from the bowl on the counter between us. I could see he was different. I could see in that split second – how was this possible? – that he saw me, really *saw* me. He had dirty-blond hair, was not particularly good-looking, although he had beautiful, exquisitely pale skin. He was dressed as though he'd come straight from work – long-sleeved, dusty rose-coloured shirt and black pants. His paisley silk tie was loosened at his neck, and he carried a leather attaché case rather self-consciously. Not my type at all.

"I've been watching you blow off all those other guys," he said. "Let me buy you a drink."

I laughed because he was so cocky, and had no reason to be. I liked him for that. We moved to a far corner of the room, sliding into a booth with a table that was sticky from spilled liquor. It was quieter there – we didn't need to shout.

"Brian," he said, sticking his hand out sideways to grip mine. He was staring at my nails.

"Luscious Lavender. Uh, the polish, not my name. I'm Elsa." I hadn't meant to give him my correct name.

"Elsa. Unusual name."

"Yeah. It's Swedish. It means 'truth'."

"Truth, huh? Cool, I like a girl that's true."

We both laughed.

"So, where're you from? I hear an accent."

"Jamaica. I'm from Jamaica. Kingston."

"Ah, Kingston," he said, nodding his head.

"So, you've been there?"

"Nah. But I've wanted to go. I have a buddy who went there a while back. To Montego Bay, actually. He says you guys have some of the best weed there. Finest pussy, too."

"So, did your buddy manage to score some?"

Brian leaned in close and said in my ear, "What? Pussy or weed?"

88

I laughed, took a sip of my drink. Prince's *Little Red Corvette* was pumping through the speakers. The couple I'd been admiring earlier were still locked in a soulful embrace, their slow swaying out of time to the pulsing beat of the music. I was beginning to feel woozy; everything seemed suddenly unreal; I was ready for anything. I looked at Brian and smiled. "Tell me one thing about yourself that nobody knows."

A fan of lines appeared at the corners of his eyes when he grinned. "I'm, well, sort of… a thief. *Shhh*," he said, looking over his shoulder and dropping his voice dramatically. "I just, like, robbed my company of over a million dollars."

I rolled my eyes.

"Serious. Just today."

"Right. A rich fantasy life, then." I started to get up. "I'm bored by liars." I don't know why I said this; I'd been planning to trot out an alter ego for myself.

"You don't believe me." He set down his drink, put the leather attaché on the table and opened it. It was filled with neat rubber-banded stacks of money, the way they do it in the movies.

"Oh my god!" I wanted to be alarmed that I was in the company of a felon, but drunk I could not muster up the fear.

Brian giggled boyishly, infecting me with a round of nervous giggles too. "Why'd you show me?"

"You said to tell you something nobody knew about me. OK. I've been driving all the way from Georgia this morning, looking for somebody to tell."

"Well, you sure found someone, didn't you?"

He snapped the briefcase's lid down and snorted another giggle. "Yeah."

The music seemed louder now, warped. Around us, everybody was moving in slow motion. "So, what's *your* secret?"

I didn't look at Brian when I finally answered. "I hate my job," which was true enough but not really a secret. What I really ought to have said was: "I'm pregnant for a man I'm not married to", or: "I don't love the man I'm married to, and I'm not sure that I ever did", or: "I'm alone here, and I don't know what to do."

There's a point in a conversation when you know that you're going to go with a man, sexually – as my Business Economics professor once told me. We were in his air-conditioned office, religious icons sprinkled liberally about, and he was giving me a private tutorial on the art of bargaining. I'd written a good paper; he'd given me a so-so grade. He put his hand on my leg and told me he was teaching me to negotiate. When, confused, I told him I didn't know what he meant, he'd told me that I'd known, before coming to his office, how I would improve my grade, that I'd known from when I'd spoken to him after the lecture, complaining about my grade, that I was going to sleep with him.

Later that night, as Brian and I slid against each other, the attaché case propped against the foot of the bed, I thought about the moment I'd known I was going to end up in bed with him. It could have been when we were flying down the I-95, doing 85, maybe 90, the air roaring in through the open windows of his banged-up little silver Honda Civic, making us sober. Or maybe earlier, when he'd told me he'd never been with a black girl before, and that he'd already begun to fall for me. Or maybe it was when he'd come up to me at the bar and offered to buy me a drink.

After we left the hotel disco he'd followed me up to my room where I went to change. I scribbled a note for Althea, explaining that I'd met up with an old friend from Jamaica and we'd gone out and probably wouldn't be back until late, and left it, and the key, with Jorge at the front desk. Then Brian and I had driven to a restaurant in the Grove and ordered outrageously expensive lobster dinners and a couple bottles of wine. Was this how Bonnie and Clyde felt the first time they spent some of the stolen money?

Then, plastered as we were, we dropped in on an open-air concert in a park in South Beach that we'd seen advertised on a flier on the wall outside the restaurant.

"Hey, I know them," I said when a Jamaican reggae band was introduced and trooped on to the stage.

I was sweating through the fabric of the cotton top I'd changed into, which I wore with faded jeans rolled up, clam-digger style, along with tennis shoes. It was a hot Miami night. I pulled my hair back off my neck. There were people as far as the eye could see, mostly couples, camped out all over the tall lemon grass. The crowd came alive when the drum and bass filled the air.

We found a spot beside a tree. Brian leaned against it, lit a cigarette, inhaled deeply. I had the case with the money on the ground, between my legs. He closed his eyes and sighed, as if he'd been tired for a long time. When he opened them again, he saw me watching him. He smiled, then looked up. Pointing to the sky, he murmured, "Falling star." He knelt behind me and pulled me close to him, gently by the waist. "I'm having the best night, ever," he said in my ear. It was funny, really; he was a stranger, but I felt the same way too. "Falling bodies," I said under my breath.

"Why'd you take the money," I asked, a few songs later.

He was silent for so long I began to think he hadn't heard me. Then he answered, a faraway look clouding his blue eyes. "Is there anything you've ever been too chickenshit to do?"

I thought for a while, then said. "Yeah. Anal sex."

He laughed. "I've always done the right thing. All my life. By the book. What did it get me? My parents died in a car crash a couple of years ago, and one month later, my wife goes and runs off with my best friend and takes my kid. Sometimes you just get tired of always doing the right thing. Of doing the thing that never gets you anywhere." He looked sadly at me. "Know what I do?"

I shook my head.

"I've been an accountant at Merrill Lynch for twelve years. Twelve. Fucking. Years." He laughed bitterly. "What d'you do?"

"Me? I sell swimming pool equipment."

We looked at each other and burst out laughing. I should have been afraid of him, it struck me. But I wasn't; I hadn't felt that relaxed around anyone in a long time. I understood him perfectly.

We drove around looking for a 7-Eleven to buy condoms, for which the surly Jamaican cashier refused to give us back change from a hundred. So Brian added a pack of Merits, some gum, a small tub of Vaseline and a bottle of Jack Daniel's – "hooch," he called it – to get back the buzz that the open air had robbed us of.

But it was too late. The feeling was gone; there was nothing we could do to make it come back. In the dark of the seedy motel room we'd checked into, Brian's erection kept fading, especially when he flipped me over onto my belly and groped for the Vaseline on the nightstand. In between the stops and starts I kept thinking about Mr Cromwell and Althea and Samantha. They would have been back at the hotel by now. Would they be worried about me? The irony didn't escape me that I'd been so disapproving of them without contemplating whether my life was any better than theirs.

I felt suddenly sick, and I rushed to the bathroom and threw up. When I came back into the room, a wet rag in my hand, Brian had put back on his clothes. I lay down on my back, slapped the rag onto my forehead, still confused about how I'd ended up there in that room.

"Hey." He rolled over now and put his head on my sternum, listening to the sound of my breathing. "I'm falling, falling," he murmured. "You OK?"

I ran my hand through his hair, strangely feeling no self-consciousness at being naked. "Too much liquor, but yeah. Just a little, I don't know. Just…"

"Disappointed? I'm sorry. That never happens to me, you know."

"Yeah, I bet," I said, and smiled so that he would know I didn't hold it against him, that the loneliness I'd felt there beneath him, when he was unable to enter me, had nothing to do with him; it was nothing sex could help.

Then he burst out crying. "My kid has Asperger's. It's a mild form of autism. He's a great kid. But his mom, you know, she ran off. Just disappeared. They're in another state somewhere. I don't know. The irony is that this money could help with my boy's treatment."

As I hugged him, I noted his skin was warm and dusted with freckles like grains of brown sugar. Why did men always cry around me, I wondered as he trembled beside me. Was there really no happiness in the world? Yet, for that one moment, it felt like we were two halves of one whole. I found myself thinking of Galileo's falling bodies' experiment, the one that said that all objects fall at the same rate, whatever their mass.

He kissed my shoulder before pulling away. "Your kids, you know? You'd do anything for them." He wiped his runny nose with a fist.

I nodded, as if I understood.

"Run away with me, Elsa," he whispered. Tears were still sliding down his cheeks. He picked up the half-empty bottle of Jack from the ground, and swigged some. When he was through he offered the bottle to me.

I shook my head and tried to smile, but I could feel the red coming to my eyes, the stab of tears closing my throat. "I don't know you," I said.

We could hear the people in the room next door through the textured walls – there were dull thuds, fevered grunts, muffled screams.

"I don't know you either, but that's what we'd spend the time doing: getting to know each other." He sounded like a child who was trying hard to be reasonable.

"What would we do? Embark upon a life of crime? A new-age Bonnie and Clyde."

"If that's what you wanted." He sat up abruptly, a wild look in his eyes. "We could totally do that. But we wouldn't have to. We'd be rich."

Brian took my hand, examining the fingers before he kissed it. "You know, Elsa, I really like you. I could come down there, to Jamaica. I'm gonna have to be on the run, anyway. I have all this money. You could quit your job. We could live together, somewhere near the beach. In Montego Bay, maybe. We could make some babies –"

"Brian. Stop. I can't." I hadn't told him I was pregnant. Or that I was married. I'd told him about all kinds of things, things I hadn't even told Eric, but I hadn't told him about Eric or the baby.

It was late. Soon I would have to get back to the hotel. My little adventure was over; it was time to go back to my real life.

Then suddenly something moved inside me. The baby. I wasn't sure if it really was the baby – maybe it was gas – maybe it was the baby dying from alcohol poisoning from all that liquor I'd drunk that night. I felt it move again. I pulled my hand away from Brian's and instinctively put it on my belly. My throat tightened and I felt tears threatening. But I swallowed them back, feeling strangely strong inside.

LOVE SONG

For a moment, Daniel Lewis remembered standing on the balcony of a Paris hotel, wrapped in a blanket, gazing out at the cobwebs of new snow trapped between the window corners and stones of the Notre-Dame. It was his honeymoon; he'd known in his heart the marriage with Marie-Claude would never last.

In the supermarket, the air conditioning was freezing cold. He shivered and gave the shopping trolley's wobbly front wheels a bad-tempered shove. He was inappropriately dressed for the weather: a tatty, faded orange T-shirt with a peeling decal of Bob Marley on the front, faded navy sweat bottoms, and dirty sneakers. For years he'd soldiered through the most vicious New York winters, but on this rainy November morning in Kingston the chill made him miserable.

Romantic '70s and '80s Muzak filtered softly out of the PA system. This did not improve his mood. Why sing love songs if there was no one to sing them to or about? What he was doing here? This wasn't so much a geographical deliberation, more philosophical. As in: *Why has my life taken this turn?*

He should have been lying in a warm bed with a woman, making love and looking forward to a traditional Saturday morning breakfast. But there was no woman in his life, nor a family. His parents had both died, years ago, and his three sisters were scattered abroad in the States, Canada and Europe. Dolores and Dahlia were married with families, and the youngest, Diana – last time he'd spoken to her – was happily settled in a relationship with her girlfriend in Paris. The handful of relatives left here – his parents' people – were strangers with whom he was no longer in contact. There were only one or two people he'd kept in touch

94

with in the fifteen years since he'd migrated, and they were really *Facebook* acquaintances he'd reached out to when he'd decided he was returning home.

He manoeuvred the unwieldy cart, half-full of items he wasn't sure that he really needed, toward the baked goods section, shuffling past a woman who was contemplating the merits of yoghurt and ice cream. She was short, pudgy and middle-aged, possibly Indian or Syrian. She wore her straight black hair tied up in a messy topknot, and a sleeveless floral-print dress of a precariously thin fabric.

Wasn't she cold? Daniel noted that her bare upper arms were fatty, like those of a mastectomy patient. It was one of those little observations he still made, even though he no longer practised. He fought the urge to look at her breasts, and his mind drifted, as it did, to Marissa. Not that Marissa looked anything like the woman. It was just that every woman reminded him of Marissa.

Marissa Stevens was to have been the Great Love of his life, but when he was a med student at UWI, she had reached inside his chest and ripped his heart out and flung it onto the ground before stamping all over it. Well, perhaps that was overstating. Marissa was just the girl who broke his heart.

Daniel felt his breathing becoming short and sweat suddenly beaded on his forehead, despite the cold. The sting of her rejection had not really receded in all the years that had passed. Still, the past was the past and he'd been meaning to contact her the six months since he'd come back home. He'd responded to a friend request on *FB*, just before his return, from Shelly, an old friend of Marissa's from campus days. He'd used the contact to make discreet inquiries about Marissa. Shelly and Marissa had lost touch with each other after a rancorous falling-out, but he'd been able to glean that Marissa had become some sort of low-profile public personage. Then, scrolling through the list of Shelly's friends, he came across a woman who had also been a friend of Marissa's. Through her he found Marissa's profile. There was no photograph, but he deduced that this was the Marissa he'd known. When he found that she lived somewhere in Stony Hill, he'd told the realtor he was looking for something in that general vicinity. He would not admit that he harboured the hope that their paths might cross. He still hadn't admitted to himself that Marissa had been the main reason for his "midlife crisis", as his ex-wife, Marie-Claude, had sarcastically put it, and the reason why he'd abandoned the marriage, his practice and the States, to return home to Jamaica to come home to teach under-privileged children.

As Daniel stood contemplating the baked offerings, he tried to steer his thoughts in other directions, but could only focus on the song that was now being piped: some Motown singer crooning in a breathy falsetto about lost love.

He tossed a small coffee cake into the shopping cart and wondered if he'd gotten everything, so that he could at last leave this icebox and return to the comfort and warmth of his home.

He headed to the nearest checkout line; when he looked up, there, standing a few yards away from him, was Marissa.

He blinked. He had to be mistaken. It would be too much of a coincidence to see her now, so soon after thinking about her. In New York one didn't even see one's next-door neighbours, and from the sounds of things, Jamaica had become a place like that. Hadn't Shelly recently posted that she'd just discovered a child-hood friend of hers, whom she'd "friended" on *FB*, had been living at the top of the same road she lived on for many years? Out of all the supermarkets in Kingston & St Andrew, how could he have expected that she would choose to do her grocery shopping here?

He blinked again. But it was unmistakably Marissa, and she swept him with a slow brush of her long eyelashes and mouthed softly, "Danny? Daniel Lewis? Is that you?"

Thirty-odd years ago, Marissa Stevens had been every freshman's fantasy with her translucent skin and cool aloofness. And not just freshmen; there were many who had wanted her. She was a social sciences student, reputedly from old Jamaican money. Tall and willowy, when she glided across the campus dressed in her denim miniskirts, revealing miles of toned legs, and clasping her folder to her well-proportioned chest, there were many inward groans. With her piercing almond-coloured eyes and sharp bone struc-ture, there were even rumours, although no evidence to substantiate them, that she'd done a bit of nude modelling for an international skin magazine. Denny Wilmore, a final-year Guild representative, claimed he'd seen her, spread-eagled in all her naked glory, on the glossy centrefold of some magazine he'd seen in a waiting room of an office somewhere. At the time, Daniel had been quite scandalised by the idea of ogling the picture of a naked girl in a magazine; it was enough to make the blood course hotly through his twenty-year-old body. These days, as Tino, the university graduate he'd begun to mentor matter-of-factly explained, his laptop's primary purpose was for downloading porn throughout the day. Thirty years seemed a lifetime ago.

He hadn't known what to make of Marissa; whether to believe the stories about her or not. Why should it matter what she did? He was sure, though, that she would not have posed for any such magazine. Marissa looked so dignified, and the women who did such things had eyes that said they had to do it for the money. If, however, she *had* done it, it would have been because she'd wanted to, and there was not a damn thing wrong with that.

Their paths finally crossed one day at the Students' Union. Daniel, on a break from studying for an exam, was reading a novel. He was engrossed in the book when she'd initiated a conversation about the book's author, an American professor who'd made the headlines a few years before when he'd been convicted of the rape and murder of one of his students.

"You think the brilliance of his work kind of negates the atrocity of what he did?" Marissa asked. Daniel looked up in confusion when she sat, without waiting for an invitation, across the table from him. She was wearing shorts and a tank top, through which he saw that she was not wearing a bra. She arranged her pile of books neatly on the table and stared at him with her doe-shaped eyes.

Daniel looked behind him to make sure that she'd in fact been addressing him. But except for a stray tabby cat stalking about searching for food, they were alone. "Uhm," he hedged, not wanting to say the wrong thing. "Well, you know, he did rape and kill somebody. You can't exactly justify that."

Marissa had leaned in, so close he'd smelled the soap on her skin. "Yeah, but can't some actions be repudiated for the sake of art?"

Daniel had adjusted his glasses and looked at her in alarm, but was in time to catch a glint in her eyes that said she'd been teasing him, and he'd smiled.

After meeting "accidentally on purpose" a few times, he'd eventually marshalled the courage to invite her out to a movie that was playing at Carib. They shared similar interests in books and movies and art, he discovered, and he'd taken a chance. The invitation had been almost half-hearted, breezy, as if it wasn't really a request for a date. But instead of the polite rejection he'd anticipated, she'd grinned, showed her even white teeth and said, "I'd love that."

He was beside himself; he, Daniel Lewis, a lowly country bumpkin, had succeeded in doing what any number of guys on campus had not – taking out a glamazonian like Marissa Stevens.

She more than lived up to his fantasies. She was surprisingly funny, smart, too, and a good conversationalist. He enjoyed being around her immensely. She lived off-campus, but they spent a lot of time together in his dorm room; many eyebrows arched in amazement.

But for Daniel, the world around them scarcely existed; he was sure they were falling in love.

In later years, Daniel would occasionally remember the first time he made love to Marissa. And that was what it was: making love, making something that he felt was quite sacred. They'd been going together for about six weeks, and although they'd become inseparable, their relationship had not yet become physical. As the elder brother of three sisters, Daniel had been raised to be, if nothing else, a gentleman, and his father had always treated their mother with respectful consideration.

So when Marissa showed reluctance, he had not pressured her. He knew the mutual attraction was there; they had come danger-ously close to going all the way a few times as they lay beside each other on his narrow bed in his dorm room, reading their text-books and listening to love songs playing on his little transistor radio, tuned permanently to *JBC Radio2*. Before they knew what was happening, they would roll into each other's arms and begin kissing. But then, before it went too far, Marissa would break away and end the petting with a firm, prim pursing of her lips before returning to her reading.

And, truly, it was enough for Daniel. He never felt rebuffed. The truth was he was a little afraid of making love to her. He was not inexperienced, but he was conscious that Marissa was from a different world; she would expect, *deserve*, things from a guy that he was not sure he could give her. For him, sex was not just about assuaging physical desire; it indicated a deeper level of commitment – and that was what he wanted; he'd even begun to think of a future with her.

But Marissa wore her family's money with effortless and unselfconscious grace; she would relate stories of her family's business and social doings quite nonchalantly, as if she thought all families behaved that way.

What chance did he have of keeping her in the manner to which she was accustomed? He had grown up poor, and had to save for a week to take her in his beat-up VW bug to the movies on a Friday evening. What chance did he have of making her stay with him once she'd graduated – if they were even still together then? Sure, he'd eventually become a surgeon and make decent money, but he wasn't an intern yet, hadn't even begun to wear a white coat – which he knew impressed girls. He knew the score. Junior doctors were grunts; the big bucks, the rich lifestyle only came later when one specialised.

Then it was Marissa's birthday. Daniel had saved to take her to a fancy uptown Chinese restaurant, but instead, she'd insisted on preparing a meal for them.

That evening, after his classes, Daniel had returned to the little dorm room to find a red-checked picnic tablecloth on the floor, with plates, wine glasses and cutlery and a fragrant bucket of Kentucky Fried Chicken. A slim-necked vase containing a single white rose stood in the centre. Daniel looked around. In the corner a boom box he did not recognise was playing *Sexual Healing*. Marissa lay on the bed naked except for another rose which was strategically and invitingly placed.

"Happy birthday to me," she warbled. He stared at her for a few moments. "Oh, I get it. Happy birthday to the girl in her birthday suit," he finally said.

When he recalled that evening, in the years following, he remembered standing at the window, staring out at the street lights along Ring Road, wrapped in a sheet with Marissa, his body tingling from the memory of their lovemaking. It had made him feel weightless, as if he no longer belonged on this earth, but not knowing that this was in fact the beginning of the end.

It really was Marissa standing before him. Daniel's stomach clenched. A Luther Vandross ballad floated out through the PA system, haunting, sweetly mournful.

Her almond-shaped eyes had lost some of their lustre, and there were a few lines radiating outwards from their corners when she smiled, but she had not aged badly. He observed the way her hair had been pulled back in the same messy ponytail she'd favoured when they were on campus. She'd become a little more rounded around the edges – not fat exactly, soft, like a woman who'd borne children. He took in her pink sweats, which looked as if they'd never been worn before, and pristine running shoes, evidently worn only for comfort, not exercise.

"I can't believe it! Daniel Lewis."

A dull pain kneaded through his chest, his palms were sweating as he stood staring at her, like a stroke victim for whom communication was frustratingly impossible.

"Dan-*iel*?" she tried again.

He let go of his trolley, turned, and fled.

In the car park outside, he stood at the door of his Explorer, chest heaving, while the rain pelted down, swirling water seeping into his sneakers. "Idiot! Idiot!" he berated himself aloud. How could he have run away from Marissa in that way? Wasn't this exactly what he'd fantasised about from the very moment he'd accepted the keys to the apartment in Waterworks?

In the days following that first evening they'd made love, he'd become giddy with the memory of the brush of her thigh, the warmth of her breath, the sweet moisture his kisses had stimulated. He would relive the pleasure he'd felt when her fingers had pressed down on his arm and she'd bitten her bottom lip to stifle a moan of pain when he plunged into her. Marissa had been a virgin. This proved that what they'd shared was no cheap thrill. She'd chosen *him*, entrusted him with her most priceless possession – her innocence. In return, he would do the honourable thing; he would offer her marriage.

Maybe this was what had screwed things up between them – he became too confident. He had only realised this many years later. Initially he'd blamed her for an act of betrayal that had broken them apart. Later, he could not deny his role in the way things had turned out. Overconfidence had bred complacency. He told himself that he had a girlfriend whom he would make his wife when they'd both completed their studies. They would both have lucrative professions; they would build a good life together. He stopped trying. For him, the chase was over; Marissa was his.

What was it about her that made him unable, no, *unwilling*, to move on after they broke up? Had he ever moved on? Puppy love, his youngest sister, Diana, had said at the time when he'd confided his reason for taking a year's sabbatical from his studies. But Daniel knew it was more than infatuation. He had never recovered from the hurt of the break-up, even after he pulled himself together and returned to med school.

After graduation, when he'd moved to the States, he'd reinvented himself. He'd had liaisons with many women – he'd even been nicknamed the black George Clooney by the women who wanted him, who moved in his social circles: the fawning nurses who kept getting their hearts broken, and even some of his wealthy Manhattan patients – both single and married. But it was still of Marissa he thought.

When had things changed? For the first few months, they'd been so happy. Marissa had taken him home to meet her family, who, despite their money, were admirably down-to-earth. However, by the time the new semester had begun, things between them had begun to cool. He broke dates with her without a second thought. He made promises he couldn't keep. Their love was surely enough to sustain them through any rough patches. When he had important exams to cram for, he was relieved that Marissa had begun to complain less about their not spending "quality time" together. She spent time with other friends. From the sidelines, he noted how she'd stopped being the cool, enigmatic loner that everybody had been in awe of, and become a social butterfly, wildly popular. Hurrying to a lecture he would glimpse her at a distance, part of a group of people walking to the library. Or she would be liming, chatting and laughing with her new friends under the Arts Faculty trees between classes.

In retrospect, Daniel could admit to feeling uncomfortable with the new Marissa. Had he felt able to, he would have confessed to being jealous of the friends with whom she was spending so much time without him at the weekends. But how could he have done that when he was the reason she'd begun to drift in the first place?

Maybe jealousy was only part of what he was feeling, a presentiment that caused his stomach to clench and his teeth to be set on edge. Wasn't it this that took him to the Chancellor Hall fête when he should have been working with his study group?

He had arrived late. The party was in full flight, with gyrating bodies on the dance floor. Over the din of the calypso music he'd seen one of Marissa's friends, Shelly Morrison, and had enquired where she was.

He registered the brief flash of shock in Shelly's eyes before she replied, "Oh, I don't know. I… I think she probably, yeah she might have gone home already."

He knew the girl was lying; it wasn't yet midnight. Marissa would not have left the party so soon.

It did not take long to find her.

The night was humid and dark; there was a mere biscuit of a moon hanging in the sky. He was sweating through the fine fabric of his shirt. Beneath the pale ribbon of moonlight he spied two figures in a corner. One of them was unmistakably, undeniably her; Marissa in a compromising position.

★

Daniel's rain-soaked sneakers made a squelching noise as he circled his car in the car park, the image of her that night, all those years ago, kissing that guy, whom he later discovered was someone she'd previously introduced to him as a friend, foremost in his mind.

"Marissa!" he called now, uncaring that people were looking at him curiously. The sight of a man in the throes of a mental breakdown was an interesting disruption of their normal Saturday morning routine.

He was running now, back to the supermarket, crashing through the door, his sneakered feet slapping the tiles. "Marissa!" He was enraged. Who the hell was she to make him feel like the boy he'd been back then? He was Daniel Lewis, the black George Clooney, a freaking catch by any standards. He might no longer have been the well-regarded surgeon she would have been eager to be seen with, but neither was he the country bumpkin she'd known at university.

"Daniel?" She appeared from the cereal aisle, frowning.

His steps slowed. He shivered with cold and sudden shame. He hadn't spoken to her again after that night. She'd tried for weeks to apologise, to explain, but he'd been unwilling to hear her reason for making a fool out of him.

"Marissa."

It was still raining later that evening when Daniel prepared for their date. He could hear the sound of the rain steadily pummelling the gravelled car park below, even from his third-floor loft.

They'd arranged to meet for drinks at one of the many hip new hot spots that had sprung up in the years he'd been away. He dressed with extreme care; he would not give her any chance to find fault. Not that he wasn't always careful with his appearance. There wasn't much one could do to avoid the consequences of aging, but he had no intention of surrendering to it in the good-natured way some of his peers did. He exercised, took care of himself; he changed from glasses to contact lenses; he was vigilant with his diet. His one concession to age was refusing to colour his greying hair, which his old barber in Harlem had constantly tried to sell him. "Brothers be *doin'* it, Danny," he would tell him. And when Obama had won, the entreaties had become even more passionate. "Barack done made us hip, Doc. It's OK now for all them white girls to be wantin' a fine Negro like you. But you gotta get them greys out. Lemme hook a brotha up."

But Daniel had steadfastly refused. He wasn't into the "white girl" thing any more – not after Marie-Claude – and if he had to dye his hair to gain a woman's attention, what hopes were there for an open and honest relationship with such a person? Good women liked men of distinction. Now he shaved closely, slapped on aftershave liberally, brushed and flossed his teeth meticulously, checking for embarrassing residual food particles, and combed his hair so the thinning part couldn't be seen.

He jogged down the stairs to his blindingly white living room: white leather sofa, white centre table, slender glossy white oval planters, white lampshades, gold-flecked white ceramic tiles. He picked up the *New York Times* he'd abandoned on the floor and rearranged it on the table. If Marissa came back with him tonight… No, he quickly caught himself. That might not happen, though he would be glad if it did – it had been a while. He was amazed at how the pain and hurt he'd been carrying all those years seemed to melt away when he and Marissa had embraced right there in the supermarket that morning. How good it had felt to hold her! Surely it was more than mere coincidence that had led their paths to cross.

"I thought you'd long gone away," she said. He noticed that she wore a wedding ring when she swept a lock of hair from her doe eyes.

He shrugged. "I'm back," he said simply. "Marriage was over and I wanted to start afresh."

"Mine too," she said, waggling her ring finger. "Marriage, I mean. Haven't got up the nerve to take this off yet."

He gave himself the once-over in the hallway mirror as he grabbed his car keys. He could wear the hell out of a turtleneck, he thought, pleased with his reflection. His slightly distressed jeans, his favourite pair, he knew would score high marks too. Marissa still looked good. Thank God. She was no longer as svelte. Not that he'd expected her to be. More than likely she'd had a kid or two. But she was still Marissa. Even better, he was sure, than before. He told her that he'd given up a thriving Manhattan practice to come home to offer his services. He was holding free clinics and mentoring young people, boys especially. She told him that, after many years in a lucrative job in the private sector, she too had become disenchanted with her life. She was now the head of an NGO. They were both better people now. There were so many things to be said.

Daniel smiled to himself, sprinting through the raindrops and hurriedly sliding into the seat of the Explorer. She was divorced. He was divorced. He felt light-hearted. The last thing she'd said to him that morning was that she'd missed him all the years they'd been apart. "I can't believe the universe brought you back to me," she'd sort of whispered, leaning forward to hug and kiss him again. He didn't buy into that New Age-y kind of talk about the universe, and he wasn't convinced that there was such a thing called fate. But now he found himself toying with the notion. Could this be shaping up to be the love story of a lifetime? Was this the reason he'd come back home?

He didn't want to get ahead of himself, jinx things, so he forced himself to think other thoughts. At a traffic light, his fingers drummed idly against the steering wheel in time to the Anita Baker song playing on the radio. He made a mental checklist of the topics he'd bring up for conversation before they got into the personal. Who cared who had done what to whom? Outside, the car's wipers swept away the raindrops; through the windshield the city was a blurred, inundated dreamscape. A not unpleasant feeling had formed in his belly.

SMOKE

I'm naked, on my way back upstairs from the kitchen, balancing a tray with two slices of chocolate cake on a good china dish and a glass of milk, when through the living room windows I see the Aerostar swing into my driveway. The tyres make a soft swooshing sound over the loose gravel like approaching rain. For a moment, I even begin to think it really has begun to rain.

But, of course, it hasn't. It is a June day with a cloudless expanse of blue sky above. In the yard next door, children have been playing in a blow-up pool for hours. I make for the downstairs powder room, set down the tray on the toilet lid and throw on a white terry robe. I glance in the mirror to see that my skin is slightly damp and my hair, still short though the chemo is over, is all spiky, giving me the look of a badass, which I definitely am not. The fact that I am still here probably has more to do with intelligent design than anything to do with me.

"Coming, coming," I call, tugging at the robe's sash, my bare feet slapping against the tiles. I give a quick once-over to the living room: the Oriental rug in the centre of the room has been recently swept; the glass-shelved whatnot is dust-free; the throw cushions are stacked on the sofa like bookends. I consider turning down the framed pictures of Simon, me and our three daughters, but only for a moment. It's too late to kick some of my youngest's scattered toys under the sofa.

I take a deep breath. "Coming," I say again, before my ex-husband's wife raises her dainty, spa-treated hands to pound again at my door. Patience is not one of her virtues.

Merrill is backlit by the sun when I throw the door open, which gives her an eerie look, like a threatening figure in a horror movie. But she is very pretty, all legs and breasts. She is, also, very young, in her mid-twenties, younger than me by almost a decade-and-a-half – as of course you'd expect someone to be who has lured a happily married man away from his wife.

"Merrill," I say, marvelling at the control in my voice, my eyebrows forming themselves into convincing arches. "I didn't know you were coming over."

Merrill looks me over briefly before giving me a little smile. She is mixed race – her limpid, doe-like eyes, slightly slanted downwards in the corners, are outlined in smoky kohl and her long ebony hair cascades down her back in a loose ponytail. The dress she is wearing is short and flirty and showing miles of long, slender legs. Very take-me-home-and-fuck-me. Probably like the dress she wore the first time she seduced my husband, who has always had a weakness for long legs. (Was the first time right after a lecture? Did she stand around, pretending to have a question about a paper he'd graded? For all his brilliance my ex lacked originality.) Smoke escapes her nostrils and the corners of her frosted pink lips when she tersely nods and says, "Bernadette." She crushes out her half-smoked cigarette with the toe of one of her strappy metallic sandals and kicks the butt beneath the veranda railing and into the garden.

I stand aside, allowing her entry. She breezes past me, as if she has every right to be here, which, perhaps, she does. That is, I assume, if she wants to preserve the delicate fabric of her marriage. Every so often Merrill comes by to visit my three daughters. I know she has no interest in them; she simply wants Simon to think well of her, the new wife who does not resent the ex-wife and adores his kids. She does not want to be thought of as the "wicked stepmother" by the girls. Maybe she really likes visiting them – who knows?

I inhale the smell of her perfume and wish that I wasn't in my tatty robe and bare feet, leaking the uninspiring smell of Cashmere Bouquet.

"I'm sorry," I say. "Did you leave a message that we should expect you? Because the girls aren't here, you know."

Merrill seats herself on the edge of the couch, her knees held primly together, and has the grace to look shamefaced, which is how I want her to look. She may have ferreted away my husband but there are strictly enforced rules in my house that she has to abide by. Advance Notice is one such rule. I have no problem with her bonding with my children; I put myself in her position and realise how desperate she must feel. But I absolutely insist on being notified ahead of time.

"What the hell do you want, Bernie?" Simon had shouted at me once, when I had refused to let the girls sleep over at his house. "Why the hell are you being such a... so difficult?" It was shortly after he'd remarried. They'd just returned from their honeymoon; they'd come around, without notice, to pick up the girls for an afternoon at the movies.

I'd looked at them, Simon and his beaming new wife, as happy as two subjects in a Roscoe LeRoy painting, glowing with good health from all that outdoor activity (and, I'd wager, some indoor ones, too) in the Bahamas. The saliva in my mouth was so bitter that I wanted to spit. "What? Why don't you say it, Simon? You think I'm being a bitch. Well, the bitch says the girls can't go, and that's final."

I was just pulling rank, Simon said, exercising some of the control that I felt I'd relinquished by the divorce. He was of course right; he's a clever and highly educated man, with multiple degrees and published books – a celebrated psychology professor at the university. But if he thinks he can psychoanalyse me, I wonder how he analyses himself? While we were married, he'd held me in low regard. Well, toward the ending of our marriage, after my second daughter was born, and I began talking about giving up on plans to further my studies.

I'd relented and let the girls go, to prove him wrong. But then, hours later, when it was getting dark and they hadn't returned, I'd started to panic. The movie was a matinee; it should have let them out hours ago. I'd finally dialled his home phone – he was the only person I knew who did not believe in cellphones – only to find that they were all there, my children baking chocolate cake from the box with his wife. There was music and a lot of laughter in the background. The humiliation of losing my husband to that girl flared again, white hot, making my chest feel as if it would collapse in on itself. When Simon had informed me that "the girls want to stay", I'd just about had a fit. "It's no big deal," he said.

"They can sleep in some of Mer's T-shirts. Tomorrow I'll run them back over to you before lunchtime. No big deal."

Merrill is looking out through the picture window into the garden, considering. The house is quite big; it sprawls out on about five acres of hilly St Andrew land. Simon bought it when we first got married, when he'd won his first six-figure advance from a big-name publishing house in the UK. It's a house I imagine Merrill wishes she and Simon lived in, instead of the bland two-bedroom townhouse they share. Crystal jets of water are spraying the parched front lawn. Sunlight is streaming through the yellowing leaves of the old almond tree at the farthest corner of the lawn, dappling the tall grass beneath.

"Oh dear!" Merrill reaches up to release her hair from the ponytail. The action highlights the shape of her perfect breasts. Despite heroic efforts, an image of Simon's greedy mouth on them enters my mind. I feel a pang; I, too, once had perfect breasts.

She shakes her head vigorously and her lustrous head of chemically-straightened, coarse, half-Indian hair, blue-black in a shaft of sunlight, bobs around her face. She refastens her hair with the clasp. "I tried calling you on Thursday," she says, almost accusingly. "You never returned my call."

"Is that right?" I say mildly, again with the eyebrows lifted.

"Would it be helpful if I had your cellphone number?"

I remain standing near the television, and look down at my toes, as though I haven't heard this last bit. The red polish is chipped and peeling and on my left little toe, almost nonexistent. I don't want to detain Merrill by offering her something to eat or drink, but I must follow the dictates of good breeding.

She declines the cold beverage I offer. The room is bright with sunshine; a thin dry breeze rushes in through the open windows and open back door. Pages of the newspaper rustle by the leather armchair Simon loved to sit in and smoke. The art-deco clock ticks loudly. Merrill rifles around in her purse for a cigarette she knows she cannot smoke in my house. This is another rule, although Simon, who coughs up another piece of his lungs each day, smoked incessantly when he lived here and still does even now, when he visits. Everyone knows these rules are mainly for the benefit of the new wife.

Merrill's eyes flit across to the photographs and rest on one in particular – the one taken on a beach in Cancun, when we lived for a few months in Mexico while he did research, a lifetime ago. In it, Simon and I are kissing deeply, seemingly oblivious of the German tourist we'd handed the camera to. I'm wearing a bikini and Simon has his hand down the back of the bikini bottom. It was a bald display of intimacy, our private celebration of the discovery that I was pregnant. Then, we had still been in love.

Merrill looks back quickly. She clears her throat, pushing hair behind her ear. "Look, I know it's not advance notice but I did leave a message with Donna-Marie to get your permission –" She lowers her eyes in a way that strikes me as intended to be seductive, the way she must have done when she was busy stealing my husband. "I guess she just forgot to pass it on."

Donna-Marie, our household helper since before the birth of our first child, had a very cordial relationship with Simon that often made me jealous, but after the divorce – and, naturally, the operation – her loyalties switched to me. I suspect it is a deliberate oversight.

"I'm sorry," I say again. I thrust my hands into my pockets and finger a piece of fabric I feel in one of them. A pair of panties discarded during Simon's last visit, which I'd forgotten about. "Merrill, it's really bad timing. The girls are spending the week-end at their grandmother's."

Merrill gives me a look. Something lights in her eyes and my heart pounds madly for a second. But the moment passes. She fiddles with the strap of her Coach handbag. "Well," she says, shrugging and looking away. "I'd really wanted to see them. I thought perhaps I could take them to see *Madagascar*."

"They saw it already," I say, shaking my head.

"Or maybe, I don't know… the mall?"

I purse my lips and shrug.

"I… it's just…"

In the silence we stare at each other. Her shoulders slump and there is a dullness in her eyes. Or am I just casting her in an unfavourable light?

A long time seems to pass until she opens her mouth to speak. She has stopped twisting the strap of her bag and is now nervously fiddling with the ring on her fourth finger. "Well, I, I don't know if Simon told you this…" She pauses, pulls the wedding ring off her finger before sliding it back on.

In the silence I hear the hiss of the lawn sprinklers.

Finally she blurts out, "I, um. I don't know why I'm even telling you this. But… I, um, I saw my doctor last week and well, it seems that I won't be able to have any children."

There is another awkward silence that stems from her sudden embarrassment over her revelation, and my guilt at my plans for her debasement. It's remarkable – this news should have made me gloat. But that does not happen. I feel genuinely upset. Why is this so? I have resented her for as long as I've known about her. I have blamed her for the unravelling of my marriage, and sown and watered seeds of revenge inside my heart. But as a mother whose only reason for waking up each morning is for my children, I understand her news is a crushing blow that I would not wish upon my worst enemy. That and, of course, breast cancer.

"Jesus. Oh my god, Merrill," I say, feeling my tongue heavy in my mouth. "I'm so sorry. No, Simon didn't say." Then, to cover, I add, "But I haven't really spoken to him in a while."

"It's funny," she continues wanly, as if she hasn't heard me. "You always assume that, you know, when the time is right, you'll be able to have children." She looks utterly abject and very young and vulnerable.

"You could adopt…"

"You know Simon wouldn't want that."

She was right. Simon loved children – his own.

"I had an abortion when I was fourteen," she says absently, as if the thought had just occurred to her. "Maybe God is, like, punishing me."

A long silence follows, interrupted by the next door children's laughter-filled shrieks; no doubt they seem a cruel joke.

I feel uncomfortable, though I don't want to show it. But I don't want to hear any more confessions. I'm afraid that maybe, in the prevailing atmosphere, I will feel drawn to spill my secrets too. The thought makes my stomach tremble. If I can see through her weaknesses, her vulnerabilities, can she not see mine? Does she detect my lies? But mostly, mostly, I feel for her. I think about my three daughters, the meaning they've given to my life, especially after my illness. I almost want to hold Merrill's hand. Something. I do want her to know how sorry I really am that she cannot do the one thing that would enable her to hold on to her marriage, which she must realise has begun to crumble. Maybe she can come for the girls when they come back on Sunday.

But before I can decide what action is appropriate, she stands up. This strikes me as brave, braver even than sharing her private bit of information. "It's OK," she says brusquely, with a shrug and a self-conscious laugh. "I was just kind of feeling lonely and looking for some company since Simon's out of town this weekend. I was just... It's no big deal. I'll be OK."

Through the window, I can see the hills, brown and scabby. In the dazzling sunshine, they seem almost on fire. The summer will be a punishing one, maybe even more brutal than the last, which saw a proliferation of brush fires all over those hills. For a good few weeks in July and August last year there was an almost constant screen of black smoke billowing up into the air, and the wails of the firetruck sirens as they chased up the hill to put them out. I watch the taillights of Merrill's Aerostar show two gradually disappearing slashes of red. Then I turn, go upstairs and tumble into bed and think about the snack that I've forgotten to retrieve from the bathroom.

Later, I'm awakened by the heat radiating off the bed. I sit up, groggy, surprised that I'd fallen asleep. The window shades are open and I move to close them, starting when a lizard slithers out from behind the bookshelf and up the wall. I shoo it out the window and head for the balcony door, which also is wide open. Below is a view of the lonely mountain road. As dusk falls, my bedroom takes on the same dreamlike inky violet as the sky.

I'd been dreaming about the person I was when I still had both my breasts. It's already been a year and still I have the dreams. Now they include me discovering my other breast gone, too. I still remember the night I realised that my life was about to change. It was a rare weeknight when my children were at Simon and Merrill's, and the man I'd recently started seeing was spending the night with me. He was younger, of course. A thirty-six-year-old divorced mother of three is only exotic to a young man incapable of visualising how messy real life is. We'd eaten dinner by candlelight, dinner he'd fixed for me, and while he loaded the dishwasher, I'd gone upstairs to take a shower. I can still remember coming out of the shower, my skin still dewy and fragrant, hair all stringy and limp and hanging around my shoulders like an old grandmother's. I'd been numb with fear when I climbed into bed, turned the TV on, and waited for him to join me before telling him I'd just discovered one of my nipples was bleeding. It was pathetic, but my first thought then was how inconvenient it was to become sick when I'd finally met someone who was smart, employed, good with my girls, and best of all, wanted to be with me. I knew it was over then, before it had even properly started.

The phone rings, jolting me. It's Ruby, my eldest. "Mama," she says, her voice soft and unhappy. "Can I come home? *Please*?"

Before I can answer, my mother has taken the phone. "Bernie?"

"What's wrong with her, Mom?"

"Don't worry about a thing, sweetheart. Jessica has the remote control, and so Ruby's pouting." I can almost picture my mother, who keeps her hair in a pixie style like mine in solidarity with me, rolling her eyes. She's the ultimate survivor who had herself survived a double mastectomy, and the deaths of both her husband and eldest child, all in the same year. I wonder what she would think about me and Simon.

"Ah."

A car's headlights throw stripes over the walls. Through the window I see Simon's midnight-blue Miata coming up the driveway. "Goddamn *Cartoon Network*," I say, padding downstairs, trying to keep the image of Merrill's face out of my mind. "Let me talk to her, Mommy."

In the background, I hear my mother gently scolding Ruby for making me worry. By this time I'm standing at the front door, watching Simon come towards me, bags of grocery in his hands. "Ruby," I say, "Baby, you know you're not to make your granny tire of you."

Simon kisses my cheek as he slides past me and heads for the kitchen.

"I know but…"

"No buts, sweetheart. If you're a pain in the neck your granny will stop letting you visit." I don't add that I ask her granny to watch out for her and her sisters whenever their father and I "get up to things", as he likes to put it, since we don't want to confuse them.

"But Mama," Ruby whines.

"Ruby, stop. Be gracious. Be a good big sister and watch out for your sisters. I'll see you tomorrow, OK?"

"OK, Mama."

"Give Jessica and Lucy kisses for me. And tell your granny to give you three for me and tell her that because you're a good girl you can go to bed half-an-hour after the others. I love you, sweetie pie."

Upstairs, Simon is lying on his back, naked, smoking and staring at the TV, which he has muted. Wild animals are charging across the screen. The *Discovery Channel*. Even in his fifties Simon is in much the same physical shape as he was in when we first met, although he is beginning to show signs of wear. The hair he often covers with a ball cap is thinning, with snatches of perspiring olive skin peeking through, and his six-pack has gotten soft. But who am I to criticise the vagaries of the human body?

The parquet floor is littered with his trousers, shirt, undershirt, briefs, shoes and socks. The way it always was when we were married. "It looks like we had burglars in here," I say, picking things up and resting them on the Queen Anne chair in a corner of the room.

He frowns at me through a cloud of smoke. "Miss Ruby being a little bitch again," he says flatly.

"What kind of father calls his daughter a bitch?" I stand at the side of the bed looking down at him, smiling in spite of myself. "But yes, I guess she was kind of being a bitch."

"I can't imagine where she picked up *that* behaviour."

"Oh, funny guy. Practising our stand-up, are we, Chris Rock?"

In spite of everything, I have never doubted that Simon adores his daughters; he is actually a great father. In the eventuality that the cancer comes back and something happens to me, I know our girls will be fine. For a moment, I think about when we met. He'd been the handsome, charismatic and very married Psych professor who wore faded jeans and sneakers and a baseball cap and stared deep into the eyes of all his female students. I'd been the fawning student he'd cheated on his wife with, the B student he'd given an A. I'd allowed him to convince me that the love had left his marriage to a wife who couldn't give him children, which he wanted more than anything in the world. We'd lain on bug-ridden motel beds on days we sneaked off campus, and I'd listened to him make plans, as he slipped in and out of me, about the graduate work he envisioned me doing, while I schemed to start popping out his children as soon as he left his wife.

I had been foolish then. I was being foolish now.

"Grocery going to unpack itself?" I ask.

He smiles roguishly, looking past me at the TV screen. "I didn't buy any ice-cream or butter. Nothing there to melt. Oh, I got your prescription filled."

"Thanks." I walk to the window, and stand there, my back to him, hands crossed in front of me. He takes the TV off mute. When some time has passed, I say, "Merrill came here today."

Simon sighs. "Yeah?"

"I was sweating bullets the whole time that you were going to come while she was still here. Or that she'd run into you while she was going down the hill."

"That would have been awkward."

"Yes, that's it… awkward…"

He snorts with laughter.

"You didn't tell me about the, you know… what the doctor…"

"Yes. She found out she can't get pregnant."

"Most women want a child or two when they get married."

"I know. But I just think, you know… A real woman accepts the hand she gets dealt."

"Like me?"

"I made a mistake with that one, Bernie," he says after a moment. I can hear him taking a long drag. I turn around to see him aiming smoke at the ceiling. "Too young and whiny. Needy." He makes a sound of disgust in his throat. "Nothing like you at all. Jesus Christ, I should never have given you up."

I feel an eyebrow shoot up, and my heart does not flop over like a fish floundering in my breast, the way I had previously imagined such an admission would have made it. I just stare at him. How many times had he gone back and slept with his first ex-wife when we were married? All the times he'd claimed to be going to out-of-town conferences flash before me.

I look at him now, the self-absorbed, aging Casanova who should have been at home consoling his wife. Instead, here he is with me. God knows I need him, though. Because if he won't make love to me, who will?

"*You* gave me up?" I say.

He is not going to respond to that. "I missed you while I was gone today," he says instead, as if the situation we've found ourselves in is the most normal thing in the world. Simon rests the cigarette on the edge of an ashtray on the nightstand. "Come here."

"You know I have cancer, right? I shouldn't be around you with that cigarette smoke." I wave smoke away.

He grins. "There are lots of things you shouldn't be around." He facetiously points his erection at me.

"Yes, well," I say, despising him for being here with me, but hating myself even more for needing him to be.

Then my ex-husband reaches for me, unties the sash of my robe. He smiles crookedly at his own audacity and slowly teases the flaps aside so that the garment falls silently to the floor. I flinch when he sees the ugly gash where my breast once was. Every time he undresses me I think he'll be disgusted by the sight of my body. But he'd asked me only once, the first time we'd gotten together after I'd healed, if I would consider reconstructive surgery. For someone as shallow as he is, it amazes me that he still wants me, despite the grotesque disfigurement.

When he strokes my belly, tracing its fan of white stretch marks that look like lines on a roadmap with his fingertips, I sigh in relief. And as his hand moves down to graze between my legs, I moan, and fall on top of him on the bed. In the ashtray, the cigarette burns slowly, smoke curling upwards, upwards and out in little flourishes. But I can't worry about that. The only thing I want to think about now is the thrill I feel from the warmth of his fingers on my skin.

A MOUTHFUL OF DUST

One moment I was defending my decision to remain here, despite all the problems, not least the ballooning crime rate and random acts of violence, and a few hours later, I was silently praying, begging for my life, staring down the barrel of the .38, or whatever the hell type gun it was, which that she monster had aimed at my head. How, I ask you, is that for irony?

It started innocently enough. Connie had invited us around to her house. *Five-thirty sharp!!* her exclamation point-riddled, smiley-face-filled, round-robin e-mail invited, *My place! Bring pastries!* That was it. When Connie summoned, we came. Not that we minded. She was our fearless leader – always had been – and we loved her.

In the end, only five of us gathered at the manse – our tongue-in-cheek nickname for Connie's home since we knew of no minister's house as snazzy – Connie, of course, Jas, Faithie, Bibbie, and me. Sweet Pea couldn't make it – a prior engagement was how she phrased it. Over the years, we'd become used to her missing our little impromptu get-togethers. She was probably sporting yet another black eye or a few bruises that concealer couldn't cover, compliments of her jerk of a bigshot CEO husband, the horse's ass I'd dated for a short while after school and narrowly escaped marrying. Every day I blessed my lucky stars for dodging *that* bullet.

So Sweet Pea was out. We weren't about to take it on, though; Sweet Pea was a big girl, she knew the risk of staying in that kind of situation and had decided, a long time ago, that she was up for it. Cynthia was AWOL, too – broken ribs from a car accident a few days before that had her confined to a hospital bed. Deb, of course, couldn't make it either – she'd just upped and migrated to Canada, about six weeks ago, *sans* the child-groom she'd hurriedly wed the previous summer. There were a million stories to speculate about, but she didn't offer any information, so we didn't ask. Then, six weeks ago, it was "*Sayonara, suckers,*" and she left us, high and dry, and that, as they say, was the proverbial that.

So, there we were, the five of us. The evening had been lively; we kicked up all kinds of hell, in spite of the missing three. You'd think we'd have felt constricted because this was a sanctified house with religious icons looking disapprovingly down at us from the walls. But, no. We cussed raucously and whooped it up, as we always did, and Connie encouraged it. Her husband was visiting congregants, so the place was entirely ours.

There was a whole lot of food: pies, cakes, chocolate tortes, those little Danish butter cookies that came in round tins. And liquor! (God, but we were still such lushes!) No fruity drinks and soda for us. There were more bottles of Tia Maria, red wine, Johnnie Walker, Heinekens, vodka Jell-O and champagne crowding the glass coffee-table (and spilling over onto the huge mahogany dining-room table) than you could shake a stick at. They were mostly Connie's contributions; becoming a minister's wife hadn't changed anything was the message she wanted us to get. Back when we were all undergrads at Mona we'd been known as the Liquid Sisters. We'd been able to drink the pants off any of the guys in the halls – drink them under the table. We loved to party; everything was an occasion for a celebration. I don't know how we learnt anything. It was so bad none of us had been able to make it to graduation, we'd gotten so piss-faced the night before.

We were sitting around on pillows and throw rugs on the floor. The door and windows were wide open; the perfume of roses lay lightly on the air. The living room's walls were a dazzling white. It was impeccably furnished with ivory furniture and polished, black, African sculptures. It was cosy and cool; gold-edged Hampton Bay fans clicked slowly overhead. Before Connie had given up everything she once believed in to become a minister's wife, she'd been an entertainment lawyer who, like the rest of us, had done very well for herself.

Outside, a lingering sunset stained the sky with rust. "Here's to the Liquid Girls," Faithie said, and we raised our glasses. It wasn't so often now that we got the chance to let our hair down with each other, what with work and family commitments. We cranked up the music – Otis Redding, Teddy P (the Man!), anything old-school and Motown.

"Remember this song?" Bibbie screeched when a Four Tops song came on. Jas and Connie immediately jumped up and started waltzing with each other while the rest of us howled with laughter.

After a while, though, we crashed. We'd been knocking back the drinks, going at it pretty fast and furious. Conversation turned desultory, but when it turned to the topic of emigration, as it so often did those days, things took a sharp turn.

It seemed I was the only one who wasn't planning on leaving any time in the foreseeable future. Deb had set the ball rolling – everybody else was considering self-sponsoring, or else being filed for, in order to escape to a North American paradise.

"Jesus, Jessie," Connie shrieked, loading up on a fistful of cookies and eyeing me with anxiety. "What about the crime?"

"What about it? I was annoyed. We were women with more than twelve undergraduate and postgraduate degrees between us. Disappointment with the turns their lives had taken notwithstanding, how could they still be nurturing that puerile notion that America was the Promised Land? Or that Canada was the place to raise their families?

"Well, aren't you just terrified? Aren't you at all concerned for Melanie's safety?" Connie asked, pushing back her heavy mane of silver-streaked hair before lighting a cigarette. Melanie was my fifteen-year-old stepdaughter.

"Are you supposed to be smoking that?"

Connie grinned impishly, blew smoke rings into the air. "If Trevor ever knew!" She closed her eyes and extended a hand, mimicking a preacher praying. "In the name of Jesus, out you demon of nicotine!"

Everybody roared. Connie continued, "But seriously, Jessica. Aren't you and Stephen worried about Melanie taking the bus home in the evenings? School kids getting killed for their cellphones. Sweet Pea called me last week and told me that Tia and Brandon go to school with those kids on the news last week who got stabbed on the bus for their cellphones."

"Hell, no," I said. "She's perfectly safe on the bus." Melanie rode the bus home every afternoon after school. Her father and I had agreed we didn't want to raise some spoilt, chauffeur-driven princess. We'd ridden on the buses when we were in high school; our daughter could do the same. She was a smart kid, and besides, we didn't give her a cellphone.

"Maybe you guys should arrange to have her picked up, Jessie," Faithie said. She got up to retrieve a bottle of wine from the table.

"You know what," I said; "it's all a bunch of exaggeration. The Opposition is hyping all this so-called violence to make people scared and secure votes. I don't know one person who's been the victim of violence."

'Oh, Jessie, please."

"No, really. Have you experienced any violent crime? Has anyone you know? The truth is, you're more likely to be raped and mugged on some street in the Bronx than here."

"True," Faithie conceded. "Sometimes I hate the negative reinforcement everybody, including the media, gives these thugs. I wonder if we give them more power than they really have."

"You mean like how constant reference to Hitler perpetuated and validated the dogma of the Aryans?" Bibbie joined in.

We rolled our eyes. Then Jas, doll-faced Jasmine, with the spiky lashes, the gap teeth and the dimples, who'd been fairly subdued all along, lying flat on her back with her toes pointed against a wall, sat up on her elbows and said, "Bullshit!" and glared at me. She popped a biscuit that had been lying on her stomach into her mouth. "That argument about somebody being raped and mugged in the US is a load of crap, and you know it, Jessica. At least in the States, there's redress. There you don't for one minute get the feeling that the police aren't capable of policing themselves and the society at large. Nobody's gunning down people in the streets of the suburbs."

She had got me there. It was true. Our police force was helpless. It wasn't their fault, really. They didn't have the resources. The problem was that the upper-middle class, with their security gates and armed guards, was insulated against all the crime stuff. "OK," I rallied, "you may have a point there, but let's face it, crime and violence just doesn't come knocking on middle-class people's doors like that. That random crime thing, kids, it's really not as random as we've been led to believe. The people who're being killed, I think they're mixed up in drugs and that kind of thing." I was on a roll. I looked around and saw that everybody was looking grim, listening to me. I added, "And what about racism? At your ages are you really about to go over there and become second and third-class citizens? Look, we have good lives here, why would you guys want to go and give it all up?"

There was a pause, everybody fell silent. I had them there. Then, as if to kick me in the teeth, the wail of a police siren rose in the distance. Bibbie snickered, looked at me and raised her glass in a mock-salute. "God bless Jamaica," she said, and quickly downed the contents. Faithie, who had recently begun dabbling in religion – finally giving in to the ramifications of her given name, we joked – got up, her long skirt rustling, and poured a non-alcoholic champagne drink that she had brought with her. "Canada's not so bad," she said, dipping her nose into the glass. "That's where the action is now. About seven people at work, count them, *seven*, from my department alone, have left for there in the past year-and-a-half."

"Canada! Ha, Canadians are more racist than the Americans!"

There was another lull in the talk, during which the music swelled up around us. "You may not understand this, Jessica," she continued, returning to her perch in the doorway. "But we all want to take our chances away because we want to secure a future for our children. It's not about us any more."

Later, driving home, I was still thinking about what Faithie had said. I know she hadn't meant to hurt me; Faith would never harm the wings of a fly. Still, my stomach felt twisted. Maybe she had a point. We were a single-child household. Melanie was Stephen's child, the accidental result of an extramarital affair, and she divided her time between us and her mother. I'd accepted Melanie and we'd gone into therapy to mend our marriage and moved on, although the fact that we hadn't been able to conceive in seventeen years of marriage was still a source of tension. We had just about given up on the possibility of it happening. Stephen and I held good jobs, made good money so we were able to save. Maybe what Faithie had said was right: for other people things weren't so great economically, the future not so bright.

It was a Saturday night and the roads were busy. Street corner sound systems were cranking up, thumping aggressive bass lines through the rolled up windows. I felt queasy, no doubt because of all the liquor I'd drunk. I'd even liberated a couple of bottles of wine and champagne from Connie's dining table which were rolling around, clinking on the back seat. Then I wondered if the hollow feeling in my stomach was not so much the drink but Faithie's unintentional reminder of how much, even in my forties, I still wanted a child.

I was driving fast, the way I usually did when I drove at night, making it to the sanctuary of our quiet suburban neighbourhood. I let out a breath I hadn't realised I'd been holding, and turned onto the road that led to my house, anxious to get home and make some tea to settle my stomach.

It really is a nice neighbourhood that Stephen and I were proud of – as if we had anything to do with its beauty – extremely quiet, venerable old-money houses with double garages, flowering trees and oceans of green lawns. We had worked our tails off to afford the mortgage there. As I cruised by, I looked in some of my neighbours' windows, seeing the lamp lights on and imagined parents and children doing family things together, and felt a pang as I thought of yet another night of rattling around with Stephen in that big house. It was the summer holidays so Melanie was still at her mother's. I knew, too, that Stephen wouldn't be home yet. I had begun to suspect that he was having another affair. The truth was I wouldn't blame him if he were. We'd had so many plans for a family when we married; he hadn't signed up for a wife who was barren. I loved Melanie but I wanted my own child. Over the years, we'd fought the disillusionment, but recently there'd been a growing weariness, resentment even, hanging in the air between us, which Melanie's presence only made worse. We were spending less and less time together, and with Melanie fast approaching the time when she'd be moving on to college – and she was planning to study abroad – we had become more like roommates. Still, as I neared our gate, the thought that he would not be there depressed me, and I hoped there'd be something to watch on TV until I could fall asleep.

I didn't notice the car parked at the kerb across the street from my house – a broken-down Nissan with balding tyres; it would have stuck out like a sore thumb if I'd seen it.

I was out of the car and reaching in through its back door for the liquor bottles even before the electronic security gates could grind close. Suddenly I was jostled from behind. In my confusion, I thought that it was perhaps Stephen, home early to surprise me. Then I heard low angry voices demanding that the rich bitch let them into the house, and the realisation that I was being held up hit me. A gun was pressed into my spine. "Open back the gates," a voice commanded. I reached over to the front seat and pointed the remote at the gate. Then I was pulled out of the car by my hair. A bottle of wine slipped from my fingers and smashed on the ground. My skin throbbed where rough hands bruised me when they shoved me towards the front steps.

When we were inside the house, warm as an oven because it had been locked up all day, one of the men cackled, his voice deep and hoarse. "Fancy house hot like fi wi."

When they instructed me to turn the lights on, I saw that there were four of them: three men and a woman. The woman wore oversized Sean John casuals, fake hair which she wore in braids, and a savage expression. My heart thudded as images of mutilation and death swarmed inside my head. This was not happening to me, I kept telling myself. This was not happening.

The woman yanked my hair and I realised that she was the one with the gun, which she pressed roughly up against one of my nostrils. The coldness of the metal against my skin made me want to vomit. "Don't try nothing," she spat, looking at me with pure hatred. "We just want the money."

Her anger was what frightened me most. I looked into her eyes and I saw the force of the blame for everything wrong in her life that she assigned to me personally.

As the men went about ransacking the place, uprooting my possessions and spitting obscenities, the woman pushed me into a chair. In between barking instructions at the men, she continued eyeing me, relaying wordlessly the desire she had to see my privileged ass dead. She had an unpleasant smell that made me flinch. She cracked the muzzle hard against my cheek, drawing blood. "Keep quiet," she said, close to my face. As we waited for the men to finish, she kept the gun pointed at my head. Every now and then she would run it lovingly along the contours of my face and throat, like an artist making fluid strokes with a paintbrush. It was so ridiculous in its theatricality I would have laughed but for the hate in her eyes. Hatred for someone she had never met before. Every muscle was tensed with controlled rage. It was pouring out of her like rushing floodwaters, against whose force I was a negligible speck. I knew then. It was bigger than me, this palpable force against which I was powerless. The conversations at Connie's played back in my head. This was what my friends had been talking about, this was what they were afraid of: the sheer inconsequentiality one felt in the face of such anonymous terror.

I sat there, motionless, my bowels threatening further humiliation, my blood flowing hot and cold through me. It wasn't Stephen I was thinking of, or the life flashing before my eyes kind of thing that supposedly happens in life-or-death situations. No, I was thinking about the unfairness of the situation, how I was about to lose my life because of what I represented, that I was a symbol to these people of everything that was wrong, and so, like most of the random crimes being committed, it wasn't really personal at all – which made it all the more tragic. I knew what it was to be truly afraid.

Later, after I was discharged, I went home. In bed, Stephen held me in his arms, cradling me to his chest and singing low to me while I cried. But nothing could drive away the image of the woman and the cold metal of her gun. I kept thinking about how I'd escaped death through the alert action of neighbours, although – and it could have just been PTSD talking – I found myself wishing that I hadn't.

At some point in the wee hours, I finally dosed off, only to awaken again with a start, a wordless shout, the sound trapped at the base of my throat. My heart was racing madly; a pulse throbbed at my neck. In my dream I had relived the terror of my ordeal; I had seen her cold, angry face, smelled her sour stink as clearly as if she were standing there in front of me. Sweat trickled down between my breasts. Stephen's arms were still wrapped around me. He awoke the minute I did. "Shh, honey," he whispered against my hair. "Everything's OK now."

Morning had begun to enter the room through little cracks in the windows, making objects look eerie. For a moment I imagined I saw the woman with the gun standing there in the room with us. Small explosions began going off in my chest. I hugged Stephen back, tight, squeezing my eyes shut. "D'you need anything, Jess?" he asked, lifting my sweat-soaked hair off my forehead. I felt his chest vibrate with his words, and remembered better times together. For a moment, a fleeting moment, I remembered what it felt like to be safe again. But the moment was soon gone. I rolled away from him, onto the other side of the bed and swung my feet over the side.

In the dresser mirror, I saw my face, puffy, a stranger's, with swollen red eyes. I looked at the tablets the doctor had prescribed on the dresser and felt too exhausted to reach over and take them. On the bed, Stephen eyed me warily. I walked over to the window and stood looking outside. It was Monday morning and the street was slowly waking up. The fresh cool smell of earth crept into the room. The world would go on outside, even if inside this room, everything had changed, and seemed fixed for ever in that change. I knew that my husband could not make me feel unafraid, nothing could, and that everything was not OK, and never would be again.

ALL THE SECRET THINGS NO-ONE EVER KNOWS

I

Ten years ago, I found out that I wasn't my father's only girl-friend. For years I'd been hearing my mother accuse him of screwing around on her. I'd always believed she was talking about me. After all, he'd told me I was the only woman he ever needed. What did I know? I was fifteen; I believed him.

What happened was this: There had been an uprising down-town, one day in September 1998. A popular area leader and enforcer was arrested and carted off to the Central Police Station on East Street, a few steps away. His loyal supporters hurriedly organised an angry protest by mounting roadblocks, looting offices and harassing people doing legitimate business down-town before converging in front of the station demanding his release.

My father's girlfriend operated a beauty salon on East Street, smack-dab in the middle of the craziness. The shop came under attack by a group of rowdy area toughs who held the staff and customers up at knife-point and robbed them. Thank God, nobody was hurt and the boys fled after they'd got the loot. Later, when things quieted, my father was able to rush to the salon. Marshall, his driver, who had taken me to a dentist's appointment in Half-Way-Tree, instead of taking me home as he was supposed to do, had chased in the opposite direction, back downtown, to see if his help was required.

My father owned a top-rated construction company that had erected the complex that housed the salon. Now, in its under-ground car park, I felt vulnerable and scared. Rather than staying in the car as I was instructed, I hurried after Marshall, afraid I would lose him. And there it was: Marshall, my father and a woman standing by a pedestal chair beneath colour posters of black women with processed hairdos. My father still had his sunglasses on.

I was just in time to see the woman – well, girl, really; she couldn't have been very much older than me – slap him hard in the face, theatrically, comically almost, as though she were some movie actress. I froze where I stood. My father was a real Jamaican businessman, which meant that regardless of how refined he was on the outside, inside he was a street fighter. I couldn't imagine anybody taking that kind of liberty him – my mother knew better than that – let alone a girl like this tiny thing – good-looking in a cheap, lower-class sort of way. She had too much of everything: yards of too-black fake hair, too much make-up, too-big boobs, too-long acrylics. Too much.

I waited for the fireworks. None were forthcoming. My father just stood there watching her sadly, like a puppy whose chew toy had been taken away from him.

"You just coming now, Raymond?!" she screamed at him. "You just coming? *Now*? Dem hold us up and rob we! An' you jus coming now?"

Then she launched herself into his arms and they were kissing, deep and greedy, rocking back and forth. Neither of them noticed, until it was too late, that I was loitering by the door.

On the drive back home I caught Marshall watching me in the rearview mirror. How long had he known about this girl? What other dirt did he have on my father? Marshall was a former boxer who'd fallen on hard times; my father had admired him and was giving him a break. I held his gaze. He wouldn't tell me anything, though, even when I begged him. I knew enough to know his lips were sealed – in the same way I knew he would never tell my father about us. That we'd gone to his flat on two occasions after he'd picked me up from school. That the only thing he'd allow me to do, both times, was give him a blow job. That after both times he emptied himself in the palm of his hand and blubbered like a little bitch, "Jesus, you're just a child," before promising we'd never do it again.

He was watching me in the mirror now, waiting for me to tell him whether or not to detour. I imagined his erection straining against his pants. But I turned away without a word. My stomach felt queasy. I kept picturing my father kissing that woman. That kiss wasn't just a kiss, it was the kiss I wanted him to reserve for me.

II

I hated eating dinner with my parents. Back then, my mother still insisted that the three of us dress and eat dinner together, carrying on the charade of being a regular family. This was non-negotiable, the one area my father insisted we give in to my mother. He told me this one night as we snuggled in bed, his arm around my middle, his mouth latched onto my breast, like a greedy baby's. "I'm the only man who will ever satisfy you," he'd whispered to me. "We're cut from the same cloth." Then he told me about my mother's dinner request.

Who were we trying to impress? Who were we fooling? Dressing for dinner made even less sense now that my two older brothers were no longer at home. I missed my brother James especially. He was the one closer to me in age, the one I'd grown up playing with when we were children, then followed around when he'd become a moody teenager. Then I'd become a teenager, too, and we'd again become close. He'd made dinner bearable by making faces across the table, or joining in, as if it were a game, when I rolled my eyes.

That evening, when my father sat down to dinner, he refused to meet my eyes. He'd ignored me, too, earlier that afternoon after realising I'd found out his secret, before bluntly telling Marshall to take me home. I would have preferred carrying up a tray to my room and chatting on my private phone line to my friend Sigrid about the guy I'd met at the shop. Some kids would be sitting at the table nervous from the strain of trying to act normal, from trying to decide how their loyalties would be split. But, no, my loyalty was always with my father; to him alone. I was used to keeping his secrets.

"I'm starving. Something smells good," he said to no one in particular.

My mother beamed as though she'd cooked the meal herself. She had never cooked a day in her life. She was a former Miss

Jamaica contestant who'd gone straight from her mother's house to my father's. "Doesn't it smell good? Adele made her world-famous rum and black pepper-glazed filet mignon."

She nodded at Adele, the squat weekday maid, who hovered worriedly in the doorway.

"Mm," my father grunted, tucking into the tenderloin. "Excellent, Adele," he said, looking up after a moment. "As usual." My mother looked rebuffed for a moment, disappointed at not receiving more of an acknowledgement for her efforts for at least coordinating the dinner.

"Well, don't fill up too much," my mother soldiered bravely on. At forty-two her looks were nowhere near beginning to fade. She was still slender beneath the long dress she wore, and her long black hair, which she tied in a low ponytail, had only a few barely noticeable strands of gray at the front. Turning her green-eyed gaze towards me, she said, "There's chocolate ice-cream for dessert. But if your mouth feels sensitive, sweetheart, you can have cheesecake. You can have cheesecake, can't you, baby?"

"My mouth is fine," I said, rolling my eyes. The eye-rolling was now almost involuntary. "It was just a filling; not an extraction. And I hate cheesecake."

"Well, I can ask Adele to –"

"It's fine. I'm not very hungry. I don't want dessert."

"You must eat, sweetheart. Tell she she's got to eat," she said to my father.

My chair scraped the brick floor and I found myself on my feet. I stood there for a while glaring at my mother. I wanted to tell her that I thought she was stupid, that I knew things she didn't. She didn't know these things because she was too busy being pretty, just some rich man's concubine, a man who was screwing another woman. What kind of wife didn't know these things? I would have made a better wife for my father.

Throwing my napkin down in my plate, I stormed off. "Just leave her alone, Camille," I heard my father say, sighing wearily before turning back to finish his dinner. "Just leave her the fuck alone."

III

Upstairs in my room, I fell back onto my bed, staring at the head of the lizard that was peeping out from behind the painting on the wall above the bookshelf. My father standing up for me at the table was nice but I craved so much more. I'd always understood that our relationship had to be a secret. But everything was fucked up now I knew there was someone else. People would never understand our relationship, that it transcended the laws of society. It wasn't as if he were some creepy pervert who fooled around with his daughter. He'd begun coming to my room since I was twelve but he'd waited until I was ready, when I got my period, before taking our relationship to the ultimate level. Which other man would have shown me that consideration?

I flipped on the TV. The 8:00 news was about to start. They were leading with the downtown story. I pointed the remote at the screen. I didn't need something else to remind me about my father kissing that girl.

I reached for the phone and started to dial Sigrid's number, and then hung up. My mouth felt weird from the filling and I suddenly felt very tired, not in the mood to talk. Sigrid was the daughter of Spanish expats who went to the international school I attended. She was the only person I knew who was as smart as me and who possessed a similar sense of humour. She was my only friend, the only person I trusted with private, intimate details of my life. The private, intimate details of my life I wanted her to know, the ones that weren't off-limits, that is.

After a while I got up and sat at my desk. As the computer booted up, I scanned my notebook and realised there was a pile of homework. I didn't mind. Actually, it was weird, but I loved homework. But tonight it wasn't homework that interested me. I dug into a pocket of my messenger book bag and found the business card I'd put there earlier. It was cream-coloured with embossed gilt letters that read:

Ronrico 'Rick' Anderson.
For Private Security.

In the bottom corner was a phone number. Earlier that day, at his girlfriend's salon, my father had called the police station and, because of his influence, a police detective was dispatched there almost immediately. After he'd taken a statement about the robbery and passed out business cards, my father looked him straight in the eye and said, "From now on, I expect you to check in here as often as possible." Then he handed him a thick brown envelope.

I knew, of course, it was a bribe.

When the policeman, a youngish muscular guy dressed in jeans and a Michael Jordan jersey, brushed past me as he was leaving, I put a detaining hand on his. "I'd like one of your cards, too, Officer," I said it in a flirty way, tipping my head to one side and raising an eyebrow. I don't know, I felt bold, as if seeing my father with his girlfriend had changed something. I pictured myself in bed with him.

I sat at my desk now, trying to conjure up the policeman's face. He was cute. Sexy in a working-class kind of way. I wasn't one of those girls who had a particular type: if the package came with a fairly nice-looking face and a working penis, I was good. Thinking about being with him, I knew, was wrong. And not because he was a grown man I was considering hooking up with; it wasn't as if it would be my first time with an older man. It was wrong because Ronrico 'Rick' Anderson was a cop, and a girl like me simply wasn't supposed to shit outside my social circle. But I figured if my father could do it, then so could I.

I slid down in the chair and pulled my panties down around my ankles before making my fingers blades and sticking them between my legs. Ronrico 'Rick' Anderson had looked speculatively at me, standing there in my school uniform. I was tall, with a curvy body that men, if they didn't bother to look into my face, tended to mistake for a grown woman's. I closed my eyes and remembered Ronrico 'Rick' Anderson furtively glancing over his shoulder to make sure my father wasn't watching before he stuck his business card in my hand. My fingers moved urgently as I tried to block out the sounds of my parents arguing, focusing instead on the pleasure that was shimmering on the horizon. I imagined Ronrico 'Rick' Anderson's big hand squeezing my neck as he pushed inside me, his breath warm against my ear as he whispered dirty things. I wasn't the kind of girl who read Danielle Steel romances; I wanted a man who would violate me, do to me what I imagined my father did to Mignonette in bed. I smiled, excited by the smutty look I'd seen in his eyes, and his willingness to betray the man who'd just put him on the payroll.

IV

Sigrid and I spent most of our senior year obsessing about colleges. I stayed over at her house on weekends and we would lie in her bed, smoking cigarettes we stole from her parents' bedroom, with Fifi, her Jack Russell, panting excitedly between us. We went through brochure upon brochure trying to decide which schools could best accommodate us both. When we'd just started thinking about advanced studies, we hadn't been 100% sure what we wanted to do with our lives or what we would study but we had a general idea. Now we knew what we wanted. "Definitely not Ivy League, the pressure is way too much," Sigrid would say, standing by the window, blowing stealthy smoke rings outside, steering them away from where her mother's yoga circle downward-dogged in the garden below. I wanted to go to a school with a good English department, one that also offered a diverse set of extracurricular activities. Sigrid was more of a Renaissance type of girl, who was contemplating some kind of combination of her two loves: science and music. Her parents were returning to Spain at the end of the year and although they'd wanted Sigrid to choose a school in Spain, they'd agreed to let her choose the place she wanted to be, which was wherever I was going.

My parents, meanwhile, didn't care where I went; just so long as I was going somewhere. To say they were overjoyed that I was going to college was an understatement. My brothers, who were both just as smart as me, maybe even smarter, had squandered everything. Stephen, the eldest, had dropped out of school, even before he turned eighteen, and moved in with his form teacher. We'd heard Casey had since kicked him out after a few years and that he was smoking crack on the streets downtown. What my father forgot to mention was that Stephen spent most of his day on a cardboard bed along with other dropouts in a burnt-out building across the street from his girlfriend's salon.

Then there was my brother James, whose elevator didn't go all the way up to the top floor; he'd been expelled from more local schools than my parents cared to remember. Finally, they'd sent him away to Florida to a school for children with behavioural problems. He had been there only one semester when a junior at the school reported that Jimmy had sodomised him. Of course, there was a lawsuit and everything, an out-of-court settlement, and Jimmy had returned home in disgrace.

And then, just when things couldn't get any worse, Stephen had come home one day, and killed himself in my father's study.

A normal family might have used these kinds of crises to band together. But my family and normal didn't share the same PO box. We drifted even further apart, our secrets stretching tightly between us.

Nights, meanwhile, I waited for my father in my room. After he ate dinner in the evenings he'd disappear again for hours, returning long after my mother had succumbed to her wine-soaked dreams, dead to the world. My room felt cavernous, filled with the scent of the occasional early-morning wind perfumed by jasmine, and my longing. I was alone, limp with fatigue, staying up long after I'd finished my homework, fighting sleep while listening for his footfalls on the staircase just outside my room, which he had to pass before reaching his, at the end of the hall. I tensed, waiting for him to pause at my door before softly turning the knob. But he would increasingly pass by without stopping, leaving me exhausted and with dark circles under my eyes the following morning, and causing my mother to cup my face in both her hands and remark, more than once, "You're studying too hard, sweetheart."

The more he pulled away from me, the more I reached for Rick. I pretended he was my father and allowed him to do to me in bed all the things it would take to keep him with me forever.

But what did I know about forever? I was, by this time, almost eighteen; still a child, although I didn't believe it then. I knew about forever in the same way I knew about love – which was not at all.

Meanwhile, Sigrid and I had narrowed our applications down

133

to a few schools in the States, with Cornell University my number one choice, although I didn't tell her. I was no longer sure I wanted to go to school for another four years with Sigrid. I was excited to be going off on my own – I even began yearning to leave Rick – and realised I wanted a clean break from everything that reminded me of Jamaica. Sometimes it didn't seem possible that I could be so unhappy, considering how much I had compared to other kids my age, and, believe me, I understood how extremely lucky I was. But there it was. Sometimes things didn't add up.

V

I started college in 2001, thinking everything would be different. I was mistaken. I was homesick, sure. But foreign students always were. To make matters worse, the pall of the terrorist attacks still hung in the air like a shroud. After the initial rallying together in the face of a national trauma, things silently returned to the status quo, the mistrust of foreigners. It wasn't exactly the best time for foreigners to be in New York.

Incomprehensibly, the person I missed the most was one I'd been in a hurry to leave behind. When I told Rick I was going away to study, he'd been upset but there was nothing he could do. I was beginning to feel suffocated by him and couldn't pack my bags fast enough. It wasn't that I didn't like him: I did. Our relationship was exciting. There's nothing better than sex that's a secret; I'd never been able to have any other kind. But Rick kept acting as though we were a normal couple – he threatened me with violence when he knew I was with another guy – as though he couldn't have been brought up on charges as a sexual offender if my father found out what we were doing.

But in those first weeks on the campus I missed him, and I maxed out my credit cards on plane tickets for him to come up so we could be together every weekend.

When my father was finally confronted with the bill, he was furious. "Who the hell is this man you've been screwing?" he shouted over the phone. Across the ocean I could hear the ice-cube in his Glenlivet hit the side of his glass.

I was thrilled when he was jealous. "You don't know him," I taunted. I remembered Troy, the boy from my class I'd dated for a week in my senior year, just to see what his reaction would be. I'd invited Troy over to study with me in my room every evening. At the end of the week, my father had come into my room and told me that if he ever saw another boy in my room he would kill me.

"Sweetheart," he said now, his voice low and soft, the voice I hoped he used only with me. "You mean more to me than my own life. You know that. I know these past couple years have been, well, I know you've felt abandoned – you know why – but I *love* you."

He was flying to New York the following week. I met him at his hotel in Manhattan one chilly October night while rain misted down in the streets. Beneath my trench I wore a black leather cat-suit that had a zipper up the front. I'd packed an overnight bag that contained sexy new La Perla playthings that I didn't even wear for Rick.

When I called up to his room, a woman answered. I knew her voice instantly.

He was still Mr Movie Star. He wore tan leather boots, a sports blazer, and his jeans close, as though they were a second skin. As if he didn't know how sexy effortless looked on a man his age.

His eyes slid down my body when I took off my coat, and his hand rested on the small of my back as we followed the maître d' to our table. All through dinner I kept waiting for him to tell me that he'd taken his girlfriend along with him on the trip. He didn't. Conversation was desultory. I wanted him to know I was pissed off.

When our dessert appeared, I said, "Why are you even here?"

He looked at me, put down his fork and squared his shoulders. "Your mother and I are getting a divorce. I wanted to tell you in person."

I stared at him hard and long. "Is that why you brought that whore with you? Was I going to be introduced to my new mommy?" Then I said, "I thought you wanted me in your bed again."

My father did not break character. He cut off a piece of cheesecake. A tiny piece of crust had landed on his moustache. When he spoke, his voice was cold. "What are you talking about?"

I stared at him, finally understanding. He wasn't here to tell me he was divorcing my mother. He was here to dump me. "All these years, I told myself that what we did was my choice." I stood up. "I know what you did to Stephen and Jimmy. You did the same thing to me. I don't know why I'd convinced myself that you and I were something else. You're a sick piece of shit."

My father watched me pick up my leather Louis Vuitton weekend bag that could pass as a regular oversized tote. A sly smile played around his lips as he looked pointedly at it. I could tell he knew what was inside. "Sweetheart," he said, taking another bite of his cake. "If I am, then what are you?"

VI

Every family has its secrets. Mine had more than seemed possible. On the day that my brother Stephen killed himself he'd come upstairs and knocked on my door. His eyes were wild but he was lucid. "Hello, kiddo," he'd said, and smiled broadly. Of all of us, he was the one who looked most like my father. Even now I'm embarrassed when I think about how I recoiled when I smelt his body odour. He'd handed me a letter and asked me to give it to my father when he got home.

After he'd broken into my father's safe and shot himself with a gun he found there, things had happened fast. The letter had been stashed away in my desk and forgotten until I was packing to go to college. It was addressed to my father but I opened it and read how it had started with them, how he'd gone into Stephen's room and sat on his bed and spoken to him like an equal. When his body had co-operated – this is what haunted Stephen all his life – my father had made him feel complicit, made him feel as if he was the one who'd asked for it. And, worse, my father had done the same thing to Jimmy.

I'd ripped up the letter and flushed it down the toilet, refusing to believe what I'd just read. But even then, I'd known the truth, even if I hadn't wanted to acknowledge it: my father had seduced all his children in exactly the same way. I was not special to him at all.

VII

Rick and I were in bed at the motel where we'd meet two or three days a week since I'd come back to Jamaica. I'd just told him that my father was finally going to marry his girlfriend, and that he'd told me I had to move out of the house. "You understand, sweetheart," my father said. "She wants to start out married life without any baggage. Anyway, it might be a good time to get off the gravy train. You need to find a job. Getting out on your own will be good for you."

There's no such thing as water under the bridge. "Forgive and forget" is just a pipe dream losers hang onto because they're unable – or unwilling – to do anything else.

I told Rick this, and he agreed with me.

"You know what turning the other cheek gets you?" he said, smiling just a smidge, so I'd know there was a punch line waiting in the oven.

I smiled back at him, and waited.

"Bitch-slapped on the other cheek."

He reached over and kissed me, pleased with himself. This was one of the reasons why I liked him so much. He was the only person I'd ever told about what my father had done to my brothers and me, but he didn't act as though I was some damaged little bird, which he knew I would hate. I wasn't some pathetic victim like my brothers. Like my mother. Rick hadn't even made me feel like a loser when I'd returned after being expelled from Cornell in my sophomore year – a bit of foolishness, which I never spoke about – and was bumming around, doing nothing but depending on handouts from the man I hated more than anyone else in this world. Of course, I did not tell him how I yearned for him, my father, that is, even now, and was unable to imagine what my life would be without him when he was gone.

And he would be gone.

Ronrico "Rick" Anderson promised me he would.

Ten years ago, downtown Kingston hadn't quite yet become the complete social and political clusterfuck it is today with its diminished offices, burnt-out buildings, dilapidated storefronts, sleazy wholesales and zinc-fronted, graffiti-riddled holes-in-the-walls behind which people actually lived.

The day before Rick would shoot my father, when he made his customary early-morning visit to his girlfriend's beauty salon, traffic streamed down East Street. Overhead, sullen clouds drifted by like bits of gauze.

I parked across the road from the salon and stared up at the window, trying to imagine what the day after tomorrow would be like. But I couldn't. All I could think about was tomorrow, and hope it would be a perfect day for a murder.

LOVE IT WHEN YOU COME, HATE IT WHEN YOU GO

Sandra Fontaine was sitting moody and alone in the darkened room, sipping wine and smoking a cigarette, her long, slim legs thrown casually over the arm of the chair. A small breeze flowed in through the open living-room windows, tickling the fine hairs on her bare arms, rustling the hem of her long skirt. She lifted her head and directed an unfocused gaze towards the parched lawn visible through the open front door.

The air was brittle. The water levels in the dams were dangerously low. Rain hadn't fallen in a long while and everywhere streams were drying up, plants dying. Dogs panted at noontime, pink tongues lolling out, sheltering beneath old cars when they could. Everyone longed for rain.

She drained the last dregs from her glass, then took a long drag of the cigarette – a slim black brand she'd discovered the last time she'd travelled to New York – held it long in her lungs before reluctantly expelling a thin plume of smoke, watching it drift into nothingness through the door. Smoking was a habit she'd recently resumed. She'd been around smokers all her life and had mostly resisted. Her father had a two-pack-a-day habit and her mother's gravel voice was, she claimed, the result of smoke inhaled inside her own mother's womb. Sandra had steered clear of smoking until university, even though both her parents had encouraged her to indulge since her high-school days. At university she'd smoked for a while to appear hip, now it was a necessity, to calm her often jangled nerves.

Outside, darkness had begun to fall, though the heat of the day had not yet begun to ease. The house, a spacious three-bedroom rental in a good part of town, had not yet begun to settle, as it did when the evenings cooled and it began to creak like old people's bones. The living room, where Sandra liked sitting when she came home from a taxing day at the office, was the coolest room in the house. She'd deliberately kept it a TV-free zone, and would sit there, smoking, watching the room grow dark, shadows playing on the walls, refusing to turn on the lamps. She didn't even mind when the croaking lizards began their awful singing in the trees just beyond the windows.

She thought about taking a shower. With the water restrictions, the taps would soon be dry. She needed a distraction, but couldn't stir herself to move. She'd been in the house for a few months but had not got used to showering so early. At her old apartment in Stony Hill she'd been able to shower any time she liked. Besides, if she got up now, she might miss the call.

She held out the fingers of her free hand, frowning as she scrutinised the French manicured tips, which gleamed whitely. Her mind wandered. A slow throbbing began between her legs and she took another drag of the cigarette. She was thinking of him. Her smoke man.

She turned in the chair to look at the phone. She willed it to ring.

Nothing.

She reflected that when she was much younger she used to be able to do things like that. Back then it had been nothing to close her eyes tightly and concentrate hard and hear the phone magically chirping after a few minutes. Now, things were different. She'd changed. Nothing was the same.

The clock on the wall ticked loudly. She stared at it.

A car cruised slowly by outside the gate. Brownie, her chocolate Lab, who'd been lying panting at the foot of her chair, suddenly sat up, ears back, and gave a suspicious little growl. She thumped her tail against the hardwood floor a few times. Then she settled back down, muzzle to the floor. Sandra reached over and stroked the animal's luxurious shiny brown coat. "You're waiting for him too, right, girl?" Sandra said softly, despising herself for talking to the dog about him.

It had been almost two months since their last encounter, and he was all she could think about. Duncan. When would she see him again? She was restless and edgy from the lack of sex. After his abrupt departure that last time, she had promised herself never to call him again.

He was elusive. "I'm like vapour," he'd laughingly told her once. "Like, y'know, *abracadabra*! I like to disappear sometimes – *poof!* – vanish into thin air." The last time he came, she'd been at home, reading, when she'd heard a key turning in her front door. He'd kept the key she'd given him. "Sandy!" he'd called noisily, as if he'd seen her earlier that morning and he was just now returning from work, as if he had every right to be there. "Baby, I'm here."

And she'd let him make love to her. Although she'd promised that she wasn't going to allow him to use her, she'd caved in to the demands he immediately began to make on her treacherous body. "Duncan," was all she could murmur when he entered the kitchen, where she'd been standing in front of a cupboard, deliberating over a pack of ramen noodles, and pushed her up against the fridge, his hand reaching under her dress.

She swatted at a mosquito now and felt the anger in her action. Just then, the telephone rang. She grabbed the receiver. "Yes?" she said, breathlessly. But it was her Trini friend, Gary. She expelled a noisy breath, closed her eyes. Gary was a friend from campus days.

"Sandra Fontaine" – Gary always called her by her full name when he phoned. "How yuh goin'?"

Sandra couldn't help smiling. "Just here, chilling, Gary."

"I missed you at the gym."

"Didn't feel like it."

"You ent feel like it in weeks."

Sandra sent a puff of smoke spiralling up into the air. "Yeah, well... y'know..." She took another quick drag.

"No, I ent know."

Asshole.

"Shit happens."

A pause. "You ent heard from him?"

Sandra rolled her eyes, reached over the edge of the chair and tickled Brownie's ears. "A. Stop saying *ent*. And b, what must it feel like living in your brain, genius?" Then, because she knew she'd probably hurt his feelings, she added gently with a small sigh, "You know he hasn't called, Gar."

Sandra braced herself for the inevitable speech about self-esteem. About how many other men out there were interested in her. She didn't want to hear any of it.

"Why you do this to yuhself, girl?" Gary's voice was mournful.

Actually, Duncan had called a few weeks ago, but she had been at the gym and missed the call. He had left a cryptic message on her machine but had not called again. Once, while driving to work, she thought she glimpsed him on the back of his motorbike at a busy intersection. She had rushed through the red lights, narrowly avoiding an accident with an oncoming vehicle. But he had disappeared.

It was insane, she knew. It was as if the less available he was, the more she wanted him. When she first met him she thought she could handle it. He was a painter of landscapes. They met at a gallery in town, where some of his works were being shown. It was a hot evening. People were dressed in white, afraid, perhaps, of attracting more heat even though the gallery was nicely air-cooled. At the bar, ice cubes clinked in carafes containing assorted liquors.

She was there with a man with whom there was a possibility of something happening although she hadn't decided on it yet – a senior partner at her office who'd been pursuing her for months. At the office, they agreed she could have been a model with her classic features, poise and finesse. For the men she was a chal-lenge. She'd been bored, which was why she agreed to meet him at the exhibition.

The man – his name was Leonard – assumed that she was going to sleep with him. He was older, and more than likely married, with the beginnings of a paunch and thinning hair that he was sensitive about. He was rich, though, and Sandra had always found this attractive in the most unattractive of men. But already he'd begun to annoy her and, even as she stood there looking at art she didn't think she understood, she'd been weighing her options. Usually, she knew within the first two minutes of meeting a man whether she would sleep with him. With Leonard she was unsure. It wasn't that he was ugly; it was just that he lacked personality. This was not uncommon with rich men, though affluence usually made her overlook their shortcomings.

Leonard twitched nervously beside her, standing too close, crowding her. She could only imagine with a shudder his sweating body on top of her, his salt mingling with hers. He constantly tried to put his arm about her waist as they walked from one exhibit to the other. By the time they'd seen a couple, Sandra was ready to go. She looked at him slyly through the corner of her eye; he looked like a little toad, a rich little toad, mind you, in his pinstriped suit, shiny loafers and expensive gold watch. Maybe she would let him fuck her for a few weeks. She felt like getting some expensive gifts and enjoying fine dining. She hadn't had any of that good stuff in a while.

He'd been parroting away all evening, showing off his knowledge of art. She didn't know if what he was saying made any sense, but she deferred to him since he seemed so authoritative. "This artist is real hot stuff, I hear, real hot shit, poised to take the art world by storm. Duncan Henry. There's huge buzz about him. Huge buzz." He prattled on, absent-mindedly stroking the bald spot at the back of his head. God, how could she sleep with him? The idea of the bald spot coming into contact with her skin nauseated her. The evening had been a huge mistake; she sent him off in search of drinks.

She was standing alone, looking at a small piece, when she spotted him. He was a bohemian, she could tell right away, looking at his bronze-tipped dreadlocks, which went past his shoulders. She suspected they were fake, but didn't care if they were. His body, looking loosely articulated beneath a milk-white linen shirt and khaki cargo pants, was enticing. Something about the way he stood slightly apart, silently gauging people's reactions, made her immediately aware that he was the artist. However, the expression on his face was tolerant, not patronising as she would have expected. She had the impression that artists were arrogant. Their eyes met across the room. Then he slowly smiled at her and she held her breath and waited.

"So?" He was standing beside her so that there was a gentle brush of her elbow against the fabric of his shirt. "What d'you think?" His breath fanned her earlobe, sending a current along her spine.

She turned to face him and smiled. He handed her a glass of white wine, and they drifted slowly down a row of paintings until they were standing before one of his works, titled "Emptiness". It showed a disturbing sort of post-Apocalypse vision of the city – she recognised familiar landmarks like the Carib theatre – painted in oranges and reds. It was a wide-angled scene of bedlam, of a city on fire, buildings toppling to rubble, with a huge smudge of grey soot obscuring the sky. In the middle ground, indeterminate figures, like a mutant species, were searching for something amongst the ruins.

"I have to be honest with you. I really don't understand art," she said ruefully. "I work in IT." He smiled, gently took her hand and led her to a far corner of the room, where there were framed works of poetry on the wall. He pointed to one by a Jamaican poet called Frances Coke. It was called "The Empty Lot". "There," he pointed. "Read that. It's the poem that inspired 'Emptiness'." He was still holding her hand. Sandra could hardly think, feeling a kind of electrical current moving from his big palm to hers.

"It's striking. Vivid … almost … shocking," she said, shyly.

"But what does it mean?" He was standing so close to her she was breathing his air. His legs were apart and he was staring fixedly at the verses.

Her heart was racing. She did not know if it was the wine but she felt warm inside, and tongue-tied. She did not want to look like a complete moron in front of this man. She took another quick sip from her glass. "I… I think it's about different things." She did not look at him but she sensed his smile.

"Different things, like what?"

"Um, well. OK. I think at one level it's about physical destruction…"

He turned and smiled encouragingly. "Yes?"

"Well, it could have a deeper meaning than just the reference to an actual physical deserted lot. It could be talking about the Jamaican situation. Maybe it's about a spiritual and emotional thing, too. – the drought of the spirit. You know, the desolation and desperation of a person, *persons*, at the edge."

144

He smiled. "Yeah. Good. There are different ways of seeing things. That's art. There is no one interpretation. Look at the last line – 'Still, there's light: how it breaks black night, relentless!'"

"Yes, that is the best line, I think."

"Yet that is the line I chose to put a spin on. See, I don't believe in the redemption it offers. I think that's a cop-out. This is Jamaica. It's a holocaust. This is how it's going to end. There are no fairy tales. That's why I deliberately made my sky grey with no hint of light able to get through." He saw the look Sandra slid him and smiled, pulling up her hand to the warm breath at his mouth. "No, I'm not a pessimist. I'm a pragmatist and I just don't see things ever being fixed."

At the end of the evening, they had, of course, ended up in bed. Sandra had ditched Leonard, pleading a migraine. She had felt reckless, giving her address to a complete stranger, but the attraction between them was undeniable. After they'd exchanged thoughts on some more pieces, he had excused himself, leaving her to mingle with other patrons. But they had played a cat-and-mouse game of mental sexual foreplay, volleying lingering looks at each other from different parts of the room.

When she could bear it no more, she escaped after purchasing "Emptiness" on her credit card, and returned home to wait, trembling, in her bed, for him to show up. When he arrived, she locked the dog up in the washroom and turned all her attention to him. She thought the sex was unbelievable; when he entered her, every point in her body felt alive. Their lovemaking was slow and soulful, unlike anything else she'd ever experienced. She had been quite prepared for primal, animalistic, knock-the-pictures-off-the-wall sex, and had been wonderfully surprised by its more lasting intensity.

After, he'd lurched off the bed and retrieved a spliff from the breast pocket of his discarded shirt that lay crumpled on the floor. "You don't mind?" he asked after lighting up, after his first exhalation.

Sandra hated the odour of weed but she did not tell him this. "No, that's fine," she said, snuggling closer to him.

They'd seen each other every day for the next two weeks.

Then, when they emerged from the fog of sex, she decided it was time to make their arrangement more substantive. However, when she tried to make plans with him, to corner him into any kind of commitment, he became remote. She purchased advance tickets to movies and invited him, but he evidently resented what he saw as her manipulation.

He would punish her by breaking dates and staying away. His cellphone and pager would be turned off. Once, she called up a radio station and dedicated a song to him on the off-chance that he would hear it. He called her while the song was still being played, angry and upset. "That's some childish bullshit!" he screamed into the phone. "Don't ever do that again." Then he threatened to break up with her. When she weepingly promised that she would change, he'd come over to her house and had rough sex with her all night. When she'd come for the last time, shuddering violently beneath him, he'd tenderly brushed her hair away from her face and, still inside her, whispered, "I love it when you come," before rolling off her and falling dead asleep. She thought it sounded like a line he fed other women, but it made her happy. The truth was no-one had ever extended such consideration to her in bed; the men she'd been with seemed not to notice that she was there once they were satisfied. She waited until she heard him begin to snore lightly before murmuring, "I hate it when you go."

After that, they had both agreed: loose and easy. No strings. No attachments. It was all in the spirit of unadulterated fun. He was a free spirit, a playboy, a bad boy who was a son of privilege, with homes both in Kingston and the country. This was all very appealing to her. No problem, she'd agreed. She had always kept a lover or two in reserve, anyway. But eventually she'd dismissed them. She did not want to be in a compromising position if Duncan were to drop by, unannounced.

When they were together, nothing else mattered. The world was a distant, unimportant thing, a small fuzzy speck on the horizon. Wars, famine, homelessness, AIDS did not exist, at least, not in a tangible way. Weekends, they lay in bed, listening to music, Brownie panting happily between them, luxuriating as Duncan scratched her belly or tickled behind her ear. She admired Duncan's mind, the way he thought. He was forthright, and that made him even sexier, more desirable. Her reality was the time that they spent together. The events that occurred between these times were merely incidental. She knew, *knew* that her one sworn duty, her only responsibility was to make him happy, to keep him satisfied. To make him want her as much as she wanted him.

But she'd grown weary of the feelings of not being in control, of being at a dead-end. She hated that her life had become a matter of endless waiting. She waited for weeks at a time to hear from him. He refused to give her his address, and she only had a cellphone contact, which she seldom ever got through on. So she waited by the phone for him to call, to alert her that he was stopping by. She waited in the darkness of her bedroom, listening for the squeal of the tyres of his bike approaching in the night.

The dog, too, had begun acting curiously. Brownie seemed depressed and indifferent. She refused to eat when her bowl was placed in front her, returning to pick at the food when Sandra was not looking. The following day Sandra saw that only some of the dog chow had gone. It had been her custom to take Brownie along when she went walking in the mornings. Now Brownie would remain at the front door, muzzle meditatively to the ground, refusing to be cajoled into going with her. When Sandra returned from her walks, the dog would race madly to the front steps and look wildly about as if expecting someone else. Then she would, with a baleful glance at her mistress, resume her moody vigil.

She took Brownie to the vet, who, after listening carefully to Sandra's list of worried observations, spoke softly to the dog for a few minutes, as if conversing with her.

"She hardly ever eats anymore," Sandra said, sceptically watching the vet, a greying man with a kind face, which looked slightly twisted, as if by a stroke, coo soothingly to Brownie. She lay sprawled out on the examination table, ungainly and uninterested, panting and staring straight ahead. Did he fancy himself a dog whisperer? Sandra wondered if she'd made a mistake bringing Brownie here. The vet had been recommended by her boss, whose faith in him was apparently unconditional. But all Sandra could think about was the exorbitant bill that awaited her with the receptionist for Brownie Fontaine.

After shining a flashlight in Brownie's eyes and briefly examining her gums, he turned around to face Sandra. "Did she lose a pet friend? Did you recently move, separating her from a friend?"

"We moved not too long ago – almost a year now – but she's been fine. It's just the last few weeks that she's changed. Could she perhaps have some sort of chemical imbalance? An obstructed bowel? Or something?"

The doctor smiled crookedly and adjusted his stethoscope about his neck. "I see you've been doing some reading, Miss Fontaine."

"I'm not inclined to believe it's a chemical imbalance," he continued. "Brownie would present with aggressive behaviour. As it is, she's just exhibiting signs of depression. It could be a result of trauma or simple depression. Are you aware of something, anything, a change in your routine that could possibly explain it? Dogs are sensitive creatures. It could be as simple as her just reacting to the heat. Maybe she's stopped eating because her bowl is dirty – ?"

"Her bowl is *not* dirty." Sandra knew she sounded defensive but this was too annoying.

"I'm not saying it is, I'm just telling you some of the reasons dogs stop eating."

"But it's not just the eating," Sandra said. "She's lethargic. Uninterested in playing or doing anything."

"As I said before," he said, sighing patiently and pushing up his wire-rimmed glasses on the bridge of his nose. "Canines are sensitive. Jamaicans by and large don't seem to grasp this or you wouldn't see so many abandoned dogs roaming the streets. I know you're a good pet mother, but it's possible that Brownie is reacting to something she's picking up from you. Dogs are wired to please their owners. When you're not OK, they're not OK. If you are going through some changes in your personal life, it could very well be that she senses it and is drawing her mood from you."

This scenario made Sandra feel guilty, and she made a concerted effort to act happy around Brownie. But her heart was heavy. Duncan had seemingly disappeared without a trace. Another week passed. Then another. And another. She felt she was losing her mind. She had the sensation, when she was awake, of being in a horrible dream. When she tried to sleep at night, unconsciousness eluded her. She appeared gaunt and frail, her always slim frame now almost skeletal. "Heroin chic," Gary described it. One day, her boss, peering at the dark circles beneath her eyes, asked whether she was ill and sent her home.

She was aware that people had begun gossiping, speculating about her dramatic weight loss. She didn't care; she couldn't help herself. She was terrified that the nagging fear that kept her up at nights would be realised and that she would not see Duncan again. What had she done to piss him off? She'd obviously done something. But nothing came to mind.

She had dinner with her friend Megan. It was a long time since she'd hung out with her, a friend since high school. The fault wasn't Megan's. Although she'd married, Megan wasn't one of those women who shunted their single friends aside like unfortunate subordinates once their "real lives" began. She had always reached out to Sandra, intent on keeping their friendship alive, inviting her to coffee, the occasional movie and shopping, even when Sandra was too wrapped up with whatever new romance was occupying her time.

Dinner was spicy Mediterranean fare which Megan had learned to make on a course she'd just completed. Starters of onions and garlic, tomatoes and eggplants drizzled with olive oil were meant to tantalise her taste buds, but Sandra hardly noticed. She sped through the main course, a spicy pepper and fish stew, and only belatedly realised that the corners of her mouth were burning. At the end of the meal, Megan's husband Patrick excused himself. "Good dinner, hon," he said, patting his stomach. "I'll have to have my dessert later." Their son, Eddie, pushed back his chair noisily too. "Excuse us, Mommy," he said in his high-pitched four-year-old's voice.

Patrick kissed the top of Sandra's head when he walked past. "I'm glad you broke away from the self-imposed exile, baby girl," he said softly, before kissing his wife on her puckered lips.

"I want to kiss Mommy and Auntie Sandra, too," Eddie said, almost trampling his father in his eagerness. He pawed at Sandra's face and neck with outstretched arms.

Megan waited until they left, then said, "Well, you look crap!" She smiled. "Sorry. I have to tell you, girl."

"Thanks," Sandra said, her eyes filling. She fingered a fork. "I think I may be in love. I can't help it. It's driving me crazy. I've never felt this way about any other man."

"You've *never*?" Megan cocked an eyebrow. There was Rex, the man Sandra had been briefly engaged to, a few years ago, before he dropped dead of an aneurism. Rex, Sandra had claimed, was like no other man she'd ever known.

"Never." Sandra gave her a hard look. Megan knew you did not speak about Rex.

"OK. You've never felt this way about anyone else because no one else has been this unavailable," Megan said. "You only want him because you can't have him."

They began clearing the table. As dishes clattered into the sink and Megan scraped leftover food into dishes for the fridge, she asked. "So, what's it this time? What's his story? He married?"

Sandra rolled her eyes. "No."

"Well? So what's the problem?"

"It's that he just doesn't seem present in the relationship."

Megan sucked her teeth softly. "*Relationship*? Oh my god, Sandy. Your problem is you're accustomed to men fawning over you. You haven't changed. This guy doesn't jump through hoops for you and you're pissed."

Sandra stared at her. "Excuse me?"

Megan laughed. "Don't you 'excuse me'; you know it's true, Sandy! It was the same in high school. Remember Bobby Clarke? The poor boy didn't sign up for the Sandra Fontaine fan club and it drove you crazy! You wouldn't stop until the poor boy admitted he liked you."

Sandra looked out through the door and watched Patrick, armed with a spray, with little Eddie in tow, no doubt inspecting for aphids. Patrick had gone full-tilt into raising orchids ever since he'd lost his job as a professor of conservation biology, the year before, in a scandal involving three female students in one of his classes at the university. The girls had claimed Patrick had promised them A's in their finals in exchange for sex and because there had in fact been some kind of relationship between him and the girls, though no proof of what they alleged, he'd been asked to offer his letter of resignation.

Sandra admired Megan's staunch support for her husband, her apparently unconditional belief in his innocence. This was the difference between them, why Megan had once accused her of having "pretty girl syndrome" – meaning that she was preoccupied with form rather than content, which was why she always chose the wrong men. Megan evidently thought she didn't know Duncan well enough. Perhaps she was right. What did she really know about him? She knew he'd grown up in a middle-class Kingston household that consisted of father, grandparents and five brothers and sisters. She knew he'd been married many years ago, that they'd been too young, and the marriage had disintegrated almost instantly. She knew that he'd quit the corporate world to pursue his dreams of being an artist. She knew he smoked weed only when he was content with his life. She knew he treasured his personal space. Was that enough?

"Is Patrick still the love of your life?" she asked. Megan came and sat down beside her, handing her a saucer with a slice of chocolate cake and two forks. She lit up a cigarette, which Sandra seized from her and took a drag.

"This is apropos of?"

"Oh, nothing really. It's just that I've been thinking about love and that kind of thing lately. And seeing you and Patrick and Eddie, well…" She cut off a slice of the cake.

Megan's eyebrows lifted. "I don't believe I've heard right. You're talking about the L-word?" She elbowed Sandra and they both burst out laughing. "Yeah, I still love him, but you know, it's different after you've had the first child. I mean, all pretences are gone. It's not like I can act all cute with a man who's seen me shove a baby out of the place he liked to call the Holiest of Holies."

There was another burst of giggles. "You're awful!"

Megan cut a slice of the cake. "No, I'm real. Listen. Patrick's changed since Eddie came along. But then, so have I. It's not so much about sex any more. We connect with each other on a different level now. I remember thinking at first that the jungle fucking would last. Trust me, it doesn't. I mean, really, how practical would it be to be swinging off chandeliers with a four-year-old in the room next door? But I swear, we're more in love now than we were before."

"So what should I do? It's what I want. I want love. I've kind of put my life on hold waiting for love to find me. Waiting for Duncan."

Megan said gently, "But Duncan may not be the name of love, for you."

Sandra knew Megan was trying to be tactful. "I know." She sighed. "I just want him to be. I can so visualise being in love with a man like him. Megan, he's so strong and sexy and –"

"– and good in bed, yeah?"

"And good in bed, yes, Megs. Ugh, *so* good in bed. He's the total package."

Megan held up the cigarette for close scrutiny. "Start living again," she said, squinting against the smoke. "There are men out there who will treat you better. Somewhere in this island there is a man for you. Get on with your life."

"I can't," Sandra whispered.

"Well, wait then." Megan took a final drag and tossing the butt outside, crushed it firmly with her heel.

Which was exactly what she tried to do, until she'd grown tired of it. She decided to go to bed with Leonard, but he'd found a new girlfriend and was no longer interested, no doubt still pissed off that she'd rejected him on the night of the exhibition. For a brief while, she even considered sleeping with Gary, who'd always had a crush on her, but she squashed this thought, knowing that he did not deserved to be used in such a fashion.

If she couldn't have Duncan, she would have no one. She would read books on meditation and yoga, maybe even start attending church. She got as far as playing her records again, lighting candles and burning incense.

But in spite of herself, she had caved in and phoned him, leaving a message on his machine. She despised herself for her weakness; it was a disease. No matter how he mistreated her, still she craved him.

★

About a week later she was awakened early by the phone. "Wake up, Sleeping Beauty," Gary said. "We goin' to the gym. I comin' to get you in fifteen minutes."

"Gary," Sandra groaned and felt for the alarm clock on the nightstand. In the weak early-morning light she saw that it was only five-thirty. "It's... do you know what time it is?"

"Listen, Sandra Fontaine. You just wasting time complaining. I reaching there in ten minutes. We could get the six o'clock aerobics class."

Sandra sat up in bed. "Gary. I'm tired. I'm not going to the gym with you. You know I hate to get my hair sweaty before work."

"Five minutes."

Sandra was getting tired of this stupid conversation. "I can't, Gar. I... I have someone here. I – "

"Someone there? Like a man?"

"Unh-huh."

"Oh, well, I'll just come in and meet him, then."

"You... wait, what?"

"Ding dong, Sandra Fontaine. Avon calling. I at you door." Gary laughed.

Just then, her doorbell bell rang. "Dammit, Gary," Sandra said into the phone, swinging her feet over the side of the bed. When she set her foot down she stepped into a mass of something wet and unpleasant. "Oh my God," she said, still into the phone.

"What you tryin' to pull now? Allyuh Jamaicans, you see..."

"Gary," Sandra interrupted him, her voice raised in panic. "Oh my God!" She turned on the light, hurriedly put on a dressing gown and followed a trail of dog sick out to the living room. There were blood-encrusted vomit patches all the way down the hallway and in the living room, where Brownie had collapsed and lay hardly breathing.

Later she sat at the vet's, dressed in a pair of old jeans and a soiled T-shirt, shivering. Gary held her hand. The vet had informed her that he would have to take blood, do X-rays.

"I told that quack something was wrong with her," Sandra said softly. Her stomach felt queasy. The fluorescent lights in the waiting room were too bright, and the seats hard and unfriendly. On the wall, the *Today Show* played from a battened down TV set. From her desk, the receptionist directed sad little smiles at them.

Sandra glanced at Gary, grateful that he was with her. His thin face was unshaved and she saw the stubble on his jaw had begun to grey. He was still dressed in his sweats and trainers and she was wearing the flip-flops she usually wore only around the house. She put a hand up to her head, feeling the messy ponytail she'd stuffed into a scrunchie. What an unkempt pair. She craved a cigarette.

Gary pulled out his phone from a pouch at his waist and called his office, explaining that he would be absent that day. Then he called Sandra's boss and explained what had happened.

When he hung up he squeezed her hand. "She'll be OK. Brownie strong like yuh."

"Yeah. She probably just had to throw up to feel better. It's probably nothing. Just some bug."

But when the vet returned, his expression was grim.

Brownie's lymphoma was apparently the more uncommon type that had hidden in her spleen. The spleen would normally be relatively easy to take out but the tumours had multiplied and grown. When he used the term "the size of a hamburger" Sandra slumped sideways on her chair and began to weep loudly.

"Yuh couldn't do anyt'ing, Doc?" Gary asked.

"I'm sorry," the vet said. "I could give her medication and you could take her home for the rest of time that she has, but I'd recommend we put her down now. She's really in a lot of pain."

She was dozing naked atop the sheets on her bed one night when the idling of his motorbike in the driveway awakened her. This was how she slept now that Brownie was no longer there. She squinted at her alarm clock. It was just after two in the morning. She sat up as he breezed in wearing jeans and a milk-white muslin shirt, his battered backpack carelessly slung over his arm. "Oh, you're up," he said, then kissed her lingeringly, pushing her back against the warm sheets as he dropped his bag on the floor and slid a hand between her thighs.

Afterwards, they sat on the ground in the living room, eating fridge-cold pizza and drinking Red Stripes. Sandra had lit candles and incense around the room. She wanted to feel there was a comfortable glow of domesticity in the scene, but hated herself for even thinking it. What was missing was Brownie, who would have been settled at Duncan's feet, waiting for him to scratch her ears, tickle her belly. The dog had always been fond of Duncan, more than any of the other men she'd been with. She remembered how afraid Brownie had been of Rex, how it had been so bad that she'd seriously considered giving the dog away to Megan after she and Rex got married. Sandra felt a pang at the memory.

Outside, a breeze rustled fronds of a palm tree in the front yard. Sandra sat quietly next to Duncan, her thigh touching his, watching his eyes dance as he related stories of the foreign cities from which he has just returned.

She watched him light a spliff, shaking her head when he offered her a drag. "There were exhibitions in five different states, and in Europe. Gstaad. Rome. I was invited last-minute. I meant to give you a call." He said this with an imperceptible shrug, then quickly continued talking about his hopes for his career.

"It's good that you enjoyed yourself, Duncan," she said. "I'm glad things are going great for you." Then she started clearing away their plates.

Moonlight was streaming through the glass window into the kitchen. She listened to the slight rattle as the cubes formed in the fridge's icemaker. She watched the steam coil from the hot water running out of the faucet, disappearing quickly into nothingness. It surprised her that she didn't feel particularly amorous, after going without for so long. She was not thinking about the rapture awaiting her return to bed. She was tired and wanted to be rocked to sleep. She wanted to wake up in the blush of first light with the arms that had rocked her to sleep still there.

"Hey, Fontaine," Duncan called. "I'm going to bed. By the way, where the hell is Brownie? I missed her."

He missed Brownie. Not her.

She watched as the water filled the sink. When she was in high school, she had gotten pregnant. The unborn baby's father was a boy she thought she was in love with, would spend her life with. It was a long time ago and the details were blurred in her mind, but the thing she always remembered was lying on the table and the doctor telling her to count backwards. "You count backwards and when you wake up, your problem will be gone."

In a moment of clarity she understood what she had to do. She lifted the plug and the water gurgled down the drain. In the next room, she imagined she could hear Brownie make a sound like a contented sigh, the kind of sigh she gave those nights when Duncan was there.

She breathed in deeply, and switched off the kitchen light. She walked slowly up the hallway to the bedroom, looking down at the faint, disappearing impressions of sweat her toes were making on the floorboards. She felt strong. Softly, she began to count. Ten, nine, eight…

ACKNOWLEDGEMENTS

My thanks always to my creative writing teacher, mentor and friend, Wayne Brown, yesterday, today, tomorrow – forever.

The stories here have appeared, often in radically different forms and with different titles, in "Bookends", the *Jamaica Observer*'s arts magazine, which, even when it was the *Observer Literary Arts* magazine, always provided a space for me to share my work.

The story "Lapdance" appeared in slightly different form in *Kunapipi: Journal of Postcolonial Writing*.

And, finally, to my family – you know who you are – thank you. I love you.

ABOUT THE AUTHOR

Sharon Leach was born in Kingston, Jamaica, She was educated at St Hugh's High School (1976-1983) and the Faculty of Arts and General Studies at the University of the West Indies (1983-1986). She works as a columnist, copy editor, proofreader and freelance writer for the *Jamaica Observer*, as well as editor of *Bookends*, the paper's weekly literary arts supplement. Over 100 of her short stories have appeared in the newspaper's Literary Arts magazine since 2000. In 2002, she received a Certificate of Merit in the Jamaica Cultural Development Commission's (JCDC's) Creative Writing Competition (Adult Category); she was also one of the first recipients of a scholarship to the Calabash Writing Workshop in May 2003; and in 2011, she was a recipient of the Musgrave Bronze Medal from the Council of the Institute of Jamaica for distinguished eminence in the field of Literature. In 2012, she participated in the NGC Bocas Lit Fest in Trinidad.

Her stories have been anthologised in *Bearing Witness* 2000, 2001, 2002, publications of the *Jamaica Observer*, in *Kunapipi, Journal of Postcolonial Writing*; *Iron Balloons: Fiction from Jamaica's Calabash Writer's Workshop*; *Blue Latitudes: An Anthology of Caribbean Women Fiction Writers*; the *Jamaica Journal, Caribbean Writing Today, Calabash: A Journal of Arts and Letters* and most recently in *AfroBeat* journal. Her essays have also appeared in Air Jamaica's *Skywritings* magazine and *The Caribbean Voice* newspaper.

What You Can't Tell Him: Stories, a collection of short fiction, her first book, was published in 2006.

Desiree Reynolds
Seduce
ISBN: 9781845232177; pp. 184; pub. September 2013; £8.99

The word has gone out that Seduce is dead, and the mourners gather for her wake. But if Seduce is in her coffin, her memories and consciousness of those around her persist. There are those like Hyacinth who have come to make sure that "dutty filthy woman" has finally ceased to be the temptation of the husbands of decent, respectable women; Seduce's daughter Glory, full of thwarted love and shame, hoping for the rescue of Seduce's soul; there are her grandchildren, Son and Loo, both in their different ways marked by their upbringing in this dysfunctional home, in search of something positive; and there is her old lover, Mikey, come to make his peace. Set on the mythical Church Island in the Caribbean, sanctity and profanity, the old ways and the new, fight over Seduce in the person of Pastor Collins and Seduce's old colleagues in the flesh, the Lampis. In this remarkable debut novel, told in a compelling literary patios that is poetic, delicate, vulgar and slyly funny, Desiree Reynolds has powerful things to say about race, class and the struggle between men and women.

Elizabeth Walcott-Hackshaw
Mrs. B
ISBN: 9781845232313; pp. 236; pub. April 2014; £9.99

Ruthie's academic success has been Mrs. B's pride and joy, but as the novel begins, she and her husband Charles are on their way to the airport to collect their daughter who has had a nervous breakdown after an affair with a married professor.

Loosely inspired by Flaubert's Madame Bovary, Mrs. B focuses on the life of an upper middle-class family in contemporary Trinidad, who have, in response to the island's crime and violence, retreated to a gated community. Mrs. B (she hates the name of Butcher) is fast approaching fifty and her daughter Ruthie's return from university and the state of her marriage provoke her to some unaccustomed self-reflection. Like Flaubert's heroine Mrs. B's desires are often tied to the expectations of her social circle.

Elizabeth Walcott-Hackshaw writes with wit, with brutal honesty and with warmth for her characters, but the novel questions how far the Butcher clan's love of Trinidad as place – their hedonistic pleasure in their holiday houses "down the islands" – can carry them towards a deeper engagement with their fellow but less privileged islanders.

Barbara Jenkins
Sic Transit Wagon
ISBN: 9781845232146; pp. 180; pub. July 2013; £8.99

"Barbara Jenkins writes with wit, wisdom and a glorious sense of place. In stories that chart a woman's life, and that of her island home, this triumphant debut affirms a lifetime of perceptive observation of Caribbean life and society."
— Ellah Allfrey, Deputy Editor of *Granta Magazine*

Set over a time-span from colonial era Trinidad to the hazards and alarms of its postcolonial present, at the core of these stories is the experience of uncomfortable change, but seen with a developing sense of its constancy as part of life, and the need for acceptance.

The stories deal with the vulnerabilities and shames of a childhood of poverty, the pain of being let down, glimpses of the secret lives of adults, betrayals in love, the temptations of possessiveness, conflicts between the desire for belonging and independence, and the devastation of loss through illness, dementia and death. What brings each of these not uncommon situations to fresh and vivid life is the quality of the writing: the shape of the stories, the unerring capturing of the rhythms of the voice and a way of seeing – that includes a saving sense of humour and the absurd – that delights in the characters that people these stories.

Ifeona Fulani
Ten Days in Jamaica
ISBN: 9781845231996; pp. 164; pub. 2012; £8.99

Chips makes no bones about the fact that her holiday in Jamaica is about using her white skin and money to find some beach-boy sex, but does Yvonne, coming "home" to recover from her cancer, behave any differently when she starts an affair with Donovan, her odd-jobbing handyman? Is there some truth in Arjun's accusation that Jewel has used him to pursue her black Londoner's dream of an exotic India? Where do responsibility and freedom begin and end in Bea's relationship with her adolescent daughter, Daria, about to make her first hesitant sexual explorations? The stories offer no easy answers to such questions, only the means to greater understanding and empathy for their characters' motivations.

"Ifeona Fulani's stories are elegant, witty, sad and brave. Their powerful sense of place transports the reader to the landscapes, colours, foliage and food of Jamaica and India, seen with brilliant immediacy. The social observations are acute, the contrasts of cultures subtly drawn, the characters alive. She has given a personal voice to women and men from the post-colonial world from whom we hear too little. This is a very enjoyable collection."
— Margaret Drabble

"Poignant and beautiful stories of missed opportunities for love, displacements, longings, and migrations both physical and of the heart. Ifeona Fulani is a gifted writer whose work is as lyrical as fables and as true as the world around us." — Edwidge Danticat

Pepperpot
ISBN: 9781845232375; pp. 224; pub. April 2014; £7.99

Pepperpot gathers the very best Caribbean entries to the 2013 Commonwealth Short Story Prize, including a mix of established and up-and-coming writers from islands throughout the Caribbean. Featuring short fiction by: Sharon Millar (Trinidad & Tobago); Dwight Thompson (Jamaica); Kevin Baldeosingh, (Trinidad & Tobago); Ivory Kelly (Belize); Barbara Jenkins (Trinidad & Tobago); Sharon Leach (Jamaica); Joanne C. Hillhouse (Antigua & Barbuda); Ezekel Alan (Jamaica); Heather Barker (Barbados); Janice Lynn Mather (Bahamas); Kimmisha Thomas (Jamaica); Kevin Jared Hosein (Trinidad & Tobago) and Garfield Ellis (Jamaica).

Pepperpot is the inaugural publication of Peekash Press, a joint imprint of Caribbean literature by Akashic Books (Brooklyn) and Peepal Tree Press (Leeds, UK). In collaboration with the Commonwealth Writers, the British Council, and CaribLit, Akashic and Peepal Tree – already recognized as publishers of high-quality Caribbean literature – further their commitment to writers from the region with this exciting new imprint.

"These are true, authentic voices speaking in a variety of tones, cadences and rhythms, hiding nothing, realeasing images that will continue to haunt us long after we have closed the book. Spoken in tones that are musical, mildly satirical, or hauntingly lyrical, cutting across various speech registers, allowing us to hear our own voices calling to one another."

— Olive Senior

All titles available on-line from www.peepaltreepress.com, with secure ordering; or email orders@peepaltreepress.com; or phone +44 (0)113 245 1703